The Master's Daughter

a novel

by

Vjange Hazle

The Master's Daughter   Vjange Hazle

Written and edited by Vjange Hazle

Copyright© Vjange Hazle 2016

All rights reserved. No reproduction, copy or transmission of this publication may be made without prior written permission of the author and/or her designee.

All characters in the story are fictional. Any resemblance to actual persons, living or dead is purely coincidental.

The Master's Daughter *is purely a work of fiction and is in no way autobiographical.*

ISBN-13: 978-1522951667
ISBN-10: 1522951660

Published by BooksbyElzah

United States

First published 2016

Other books by Vjange Hazle

Mariana (2007 & 2015)
country gal a foreign-vol. 1 (2004 & 2014)
country gal a foreign-vol. 2 (2014)
country gal a foreign-vol. 3(2015)
The Dark Side of Darkness (2008 & 2015))
My Father and Other Disasters (2010)
The Scent of a Man (2014)
Duppy Unda di Bridge and Other Tales (2015)
A Thin Volume of Poetry Due to Writer's Block (2015)
Abby's Secret (2015)
My Little Red Book on Parenting (2015)
My Little Red Book on Getting Older (2015)

The Master's Daughter   Vjange Hazle

To the Forgotten ones;

this is your story

Acknowledgments

In the 1750s, a young man named Thomas Thistlewood arrived in the British colony of Jamaica and eventually came to own a property in Westmoreland called Breadnut Island Pen. It is to him that we owe a depth of gratitude for his documentation of daily plantation life in the 1700s; a life that was perhaps just as challenging for the white male trying to carve out a space for himself in history as it was for the enslaved who had no options. The integration of master and slave effectively blurred the racial and social lines in that society as both struggled for survival in the infant days of colonial slavery. The result of this was more than just the creation of a new racial structure; a whole society was formed that was uniquely West Indian.

It is from perusal of some of Thistlewood's writings that I learned that a property called Flamstead, with which my family name is associated, was not a pleasant place to visit. Apparently, it was a swampy place and challenging to manage. I can only imagine it was not a healthy place for either master or slave.

I also owe eternal gratitude to the other real people in my life who went on the journey through history with me.

Thanks to my sister Muffett, who had the task of reading the first draft, for giving me valuable feedback and suggestions on the plot, and her co-worker who literally wept at the reality of slavery (I must have done something right).

My thanks to fellow writer Dantie Smith-Brown for reading a draft and giving feedback that made me believe in the 'realness' of the characters.

My heartfelt appreciation to my professors at Central Connecticut State University, who encouraged me in my exploration of the West Indian Creole, a journey on which I encountered the mulatto and the in-between space she/he occupied in the colony in the 17th and 18th centuries.

To my faithful readers who patiently (or impatiently) wait for the next one, I give you all my love and thanks. Keep reading.

        --Vjange

Prelude

Western Jamaica, British West Indies, 1760

The wailing of the newborn filled the quiet of the night. Mary lay on her back, staring up at the ceiling of the hut, the lamplight playing with her dark features. The voice of Rosanna the midwife seemed to come from a great distance, cajoling and comforting as she wiped the baby boy's shiny, dark skin clean. Below her waist, Mary felt nothing, as if the pain of a few hours before up to this moment had never existed. High above, the stars seemed to dance as they peeped through the thatch roof of the hut at her. She turned her head to watch Rosanna as the woman tried to quiet the infant. The words she sang to the baby were from the place where he had been conceived, a place that Mary wondered if her child would ever see. It was the place where her own name was *Afua*.

Rosanna placed the infant next to the new mother on the narrow cot and helped Mary to sit up. The baby automatically reached for Mary's full breasts as Rosanna placed him in his mother's arms. Mary felt the tears streaming down her face as she stared at the round face of the boy who would someday stand tall like his father; a father he would never know. He would have been a chief someday, but now, in this strange land that was not her home, she wondered what he would be.

"She awright?" a male voice called from outside.

"Yes, Quaco, come inside come see you boy child," Rosanna

answered, opening the roughly hewn door to admit the tall, dark man who had to bow slightly before he could stand up straight in the room.

Rosanna left the darkness of the slave quarters, a torch lighting her way to the Great House where another woman waited. Mary and Quaco and their newly born child would be alright.

Quaco stood looking at the young woman on the bed, his cloth hat folded in his big hands. It was twisted and dirty from the wringing he had given it as he had waited outside for Mary to be delivered of her burden. The baby pulled at her breast. Quaco looked at the ground.

"Mary, you awright?" he asked to the dirt floor, his language still on his tongue.

"Yes, Quaco."

"Me sleep pon floor."

"Uhum," she grunted back at him, her voice gentle in its tiredness.

Quaco folded himself on the dirt floor next to the cot and closed his eyes. In the still night, he could hear the sucking and sounds of contentment of the infant. He had not looked at the baby. He knew he would not find himself in those eyes when they opened. But he had promised Mary that he would call the child Samson.

The smell of the earth was strong in his nostrils, the new earth he must now trod, head bowed, answering to a Massa. Quaco folded his arms and rested his head against the crumpled hat. His eyes closed and soon he drifted off into a labor-induced sleep. Morning would come soon.

Mary heard his snore and a small smile came to her lips. Quaco.

Across the dark passage, their eyes had met in the hold of the ship. Her sickness had not been just because of the roiling sea or the stench of bodies and their issue for what seemed a never-ending journey. Quaco's eyes had looked upon her with more than kindness as the light filtered through the darkness of the hold. When they were ordered on deck, some occupants of the dark belly did not move; could not move. Their corpses were thrown overboard to the watery deep. No one beat the drums for them.

Quaco had hidden food and fed her and she had watched his sturdy, muscular frame become gaunt and ashen as time passed. Her eyes had pleaded to him, 'no', but as her belly began to swell and the hungry child inside of her called for more, she had smiled her thanks. The man in the black coat had seen her one day as they had stood on the deck, her head hanging, trying to hide her shame, and had singled her out. He had ordered her fed more than the others. The gods must have smiled down on her and the child she carried. Her child was born for a reason.

The baby fell asleep on her breast. Gently, Mary lifted him and placed him on the narrow bed next to her. Feeling was slowly returning to her legs and she felt a slight throbbing between her thighs. Her breasts hurt from the baby's sucking. She lay back. It felt so strange in the silence of the night with no other familiar voices or soft snores and sleepy shoves and kicks from her brothers and sisters or the sounds of her mother's shuffles as she watched over their safety through the night. The only sounds were the call of the creatures of the night and the gentle snores of the man who lay on the floor, still the stranger who had treated her as a friend.

Rosanna heard the front door close behind her as she ventured further into the Great House. Candles burned, casting shadows around the room. She followed the figure of the man who led the way to the small room next to the library. No words were exchanged as she hurried toward the dark-skinned young woman who lay prostrate on the narrow bed, the swell of her belly protruding beneath her nightgown and the sheets.

"Isabella," Rosanna greeted as the man silently slipped out, closing the door behind him.

Isabella looked up, her pain-filled eyes expressing her gratitude. A sharp pain engulfed her belly once more and she stifled the cry it was forcing from her. She tried breathing but it felt like her breath was being choked off. She wanted to curse someone, to lash out at the man who had brought her to this.

"Me think you wasn't going come, Miss Rosanna," Isabella

said once the pain subsided.

At seventeen, Isabella had seen enough of women in pain as they brought forth new life into the world. Her own mother Ella had only a few months before delivered herself of a baby boy, born in the dark of night, and Isabella had been there to wipe the sweat from her brow as she hollered. But, seeing and feeling were two different things.

Rosanna mopped Isabella's brow with a cloth.

"Don't worry yourself, Isabella," Rosanna reassured. "How Miss Ella and the baby?"

"Him hardly want suckle, ma'am," Isabella replied, her young brow furrowed.

Pain ripped across her belly again and Isabella shouted in agony. She felt the urge to use the latrine.

Rosanna lifted Isabella's nightdress and parted her legs.

As her pain increased, Isabella wondered when it was going to end. Her mother's last child had come sliding out as if he knew the world was made for him. As if he knew that, of her nine, he would be one to survive like his sister Isabella.

The others had not lived through the night. They had sputtered where they lay and had not seen the light of morning. Isabella remembered the first time she had to take the still infant her mother had just given birth to, wrapped in coarse cloth and bury it in the darkness of the night.

For a long time she could tell where each of them was buried, four girl children and three boy children who did not have names. Maybe they knew and did not want to come into the world. Maybe they already knew the heat of the sun and the feel of lashes on their backs that was their reward for being born the child of a slave woman.

The pain was coming faster and getting harder to bear. Isabella felt her mind must surely be lost as wave after wave swept through her and sweat poured from her body. Rosanna's voice telling her to push seemed so far away.

A muffled sound penetrated her consciousness and Isabella became aware that the pains had ceased and her body felt a sudden relief. A faint cry reached her ears. Rosanna was wiping the small figure that whimpered. It then let out a loud cry and Isabella felt her heart leap. Her brothers and sisters had not cried at their birth and that is how she knew her baby was here to stay.

Quaco stirred before the sun rose. He dusted his hat and brushed his hands down his lean body to rid his clothes of any accumulated dirt. The sound of the *korchee* was followed by the noises of people rising and moving about. Quaco glanced at the sleeping Mary. His Afua. Her face was so still after her ordeal. The baby boy sucked on his small thumb. Quaco hurried out to meet the day and the backbreaking work that was now part of his lot.

St. Mary's Parish, Jamaica, British West Indies, 1760

The dark figures did not need the light as they marched. Light was dangerous for the Coramantees as they proceeded to Ballard's Valley. Behind them, they had left a wave of destruction. The plantations at Trinity and Frontier were still sleeping when they attacked. Fort Haldane had provided them all the weapons they needed and Esher and Heywood were easy to overpower. The smell of burning sugarcane filled the air and the fires danced into the night sky up to heaven.

Tacky, their chieftain paused to wipe his brow. The night had been a long one and the scent of spilled blood filled his nostrils. It was on his hands and on his skin; in his hair. He could not think of that now. His own Coramantee blood ran stronger that his pity for the white people he and his band had slaughtered. Man, woman, child, they were all the same: the white child he had watched being born, already a whip in hand, would eventually become his father; a master. The white woman spat in the food she offered you to eat while ordering more lashes because you were too slow in bringing the food.

Looking up at the sky he knew morning would come soon. A sudden light flashed across the sky. Tacky could almost hear the sound it made as it disappeared with its long tail darting behind like a harbinger. Its colors were like a rainbow against the dark sky. A slight chill rushed through the chieftain's body on which the sweat had dried. He was not tired. He felt alive; his freedom lay before him. It was time.

As dawn approached, the numbers grew. The people like their leader, smelled freedom. For too long someone had been their master. The Akan were not meant to be enslaved.

Ballard's Valley was awake and alive. Negroes were jubilant in their voices and in the way they walked like men. They danced to the beat of the *djembe*, their feet pounding the earth they had toiled for another with nothing to claim for themselves; memories of a land they were slowly forgetting becoming more distant to their minds.

The sound of squealing pigs as they were being slaughtered for celebration mingled with the voices that sang one to another:

Freedom!

The cry came to Tacky's ears. Never was there a sweeter sound. Finally. *Freedom!*

Forrest Estate, Westmoreland Parish, Jamaica, British West Indies, 1760

The scent of burning cane filled Caesar's nostrils. His sinewy form clad only in short cut trousers stood dark against the blazing fields and houses. His weapon still smoked from its recent firing. He could hear the raised voices around him as commands were issued. The surprised gasps and screams of the dying echoed in his head.

Around him were Coramantee men and women marching like warriors, the taste of blood still on their tongues, vengeance still in their thoughts. In their wake was massive destruction of life and property as they headed to the woods to set up their fortress. Those Negroes who had traitorously chosen not to join them had been themselves dispatched of. *Freedom for them*, Caesar mused.

The numbers swelled when some twenty, armed by their trusting master to help defend his plantation, respectfully left him to join the enslaved rebels. As they had surrounded the plantation house, their sudden appearance had taken Smith, Captain Forrest's attorney and his dinner companions by surprise. The whites had heard about but had not expected that, far removed from Tacky's rebellion on the other side of the island, these Negroes of Westmoreland would join the uprising; especially given the outcomes: the execution of their fearless leaders and companions. Furthermore, they were benevolent masters who saw to their slaves' every need.

Caesar shook his wooly head. *Good masters*!

Freedom! The word rang out across the encampment. Caesar hurried to his newly constructed hut, walking by the French Negroes of Guadaloupe who had been unafraid to slaughter; it was what they had been trained to do and what had had them shipped to the island in the first place. They had been bought by Captain Forrest to work as slaves on his plantation. If only Forrest had known.

Caesar lowered himself opposite his brother Hercules who sat on a stone by the door sharpening his bill. The weapon he preferred was no longer an instrument of cultivation in his hands. Its blade winked at him as if in a conspiracy. Tonight they wait for the militia. They will come. They must come. And, when they did, they were ready.

The old Coramantee sniffed the air cautiously. His eyes were red in the darkness of the night, his body shimmering as if oiled, reflecting the light of the fire by which he sat. He too was ready. Let them come. Let them come. He would catch the bullets and throw them back at the enemies. He did not need parrot's beaks, feathers or grave dirt. His body was his instrument, his weapon. The glow of his eyes would light the way to freedom for his people.

Jamaica, British West Indies, 1761

Quaco sat watching Samson as the boy played in the dirt, a tattered shirt many times his size covering his small body. Quaco tested the blade of the bill he was sharpening. It was Saturday but it was no day of rest for the slaves on Duncan Henderson's Greenrock Estate. Mary hoed at the ground. Her child was still too young to eat yam but she often gave him a taste of a boiled finger of banana she crushed and mixed with coconut oil. The boy was growing and soon he was going to want more than her milk. She glanced at Quaco. He seemed deep in his thoughts.

Quaco was recalling the night a year ago when he had joined fellow Coramantees in the darkness of the night. Mary had begged him not to go. Mr. Henderson had not done them any wrong. He fed and clothed them. They had their own small wattle and daub hut. They could plant a little and reap enough to fill their bellies. Henderson was most often away and his overseer cared more about felling the women than what the slaves did when they were not in the fields. In some ways, they were free.

Quaco had looked at Mary as if at a senseless woman. To think he had thought her of warrior blood. Did she want to remain a slave for all her life? And, what of her young son Samson? Did she want him to become just another slave to be shifted and sold, branded and beaten like they had been?

What would they do if they freed themselves, Mary asked.

How would they live? *Where* would they live? The militia would surely come and kill them all, she moaned.

The militia *had* come. First, they had been hurriedly gathered and sent in pursuit of the rebels. But, they had not been prepared for the Coramantees who had ambushed and defeated them, sending them running in terror at their mighty force. Watching Caesar and Hercules rise to their full height and the old Coramantee standing tall amongst them, his body seeming to radiate a light that was their guide, had given Quaco the courage he needed to wield his bill from one side to the next. It was as if Tacky had returned and possessed them all that night. The militia ran, falling over precipices. Quaco could still hear their cries as they tumbled to their deaths. In the height of the battle, Quaco had felt a presence and he glanced to his side.

Mary, baby Samson strapped to her back by a wide strip of cloth tied across her breast, held a pistol and aimed. The militiaman fell, arms flailing as if drunk. Mary, ready to die rather than remain a slave. Mary, ready for her child to die rather than grow up to be a slave. Mary, warrior woman.

That night he held Mary close to his bosom in the narrow bed. Her warm young body against his stirred him. Until tonight, he had slept on the floor, watching over her from where he lay, waiting for the soft sound of her breathing to tell him she had fallen into slumber. For all everyone knew, she was his wife.

Quaco's hand came to her face, feeling the smoothness beneath his palm. She smelled of earth and sweat like he himself did.

They had hurried back to the plantation after the slaughter, praying that they would not be caught. Only Isabella, the young cook was about, walking with her restless mulatto child in her arms in the still night, hoping the little girl would go to sleep. Their eyes met in the darkness but Isabella's eyes glazed over until they rested again on her baby and her voice softly cooed a lullaby. Quickly, she wrapped her child up in the blanket and hurried back into the Great House. Maybe tomorrow things would be different. Maybe tomorrow they would all be free.

Only, freedom did not come. Only laws that told them they could not gather together or leave the plantations as they wanted. And laws that gave white people even more power over their slaves. And laws that said Negroes pretending to have communication with the Devil would be put to death or transported. Quaco thought of Caesar and Hercules and the old Coramantee who threw back the bullets he had caught, scattering the militia. Their heads had rolled. *Free at last*!

In the darkness Quaco could sense Mary's eyes searching his and knew a smile was on her face. His hands moved down her body, its curves now rounded by motherhood. He felt her tremble and the stirring in his loins increased.

His lips came to touch hers and he heard her breath catch. Mary's body moved into his, fitting against his hardness. He wrapped his arms around her body, pulling her close.

"Afua," he called in a tongue he was beginning to forget.

The Master's Daughter	Vjange Hazle

Jamaica, British West Indies 1762

The little girl stooped in the dust, her curly golden-brown hair short on her head. Around her, chickens pecked at the grassy patch, scratching and fussing. Cook stood at the door of the cookhouse, a *yabba* in one hand as she surveyed the brood. One fleshy arm stood akimbo.

"Chee-chee-chee," Cook called loudly as she grabbed a fistful of the stale food in her chubby hand and threw it wide across a patch of bald earth.

The chickens dashed forward, creating a small whirlpool of dust as they jostled each other for the prize. The little girl's plump hand reached for a fluffy baby chicken that was beginning to run after its mother who had joined the melee. Suddenly, the hen whirled at the sound of her chick's cry. Head low and wings of ruffled feathers spread, she headed for the child whose hand closed in on the feathered softness. Cook swooped up the child before the hen could reach her and the little girl dropped the throbbing ball of feathers as Cook placed her firmly on her broad hip.

The little girl looked up into the broad black face of the young woman who had saved her, her grey eyes searching the dark brown almost black and mysterious slanted ones. As Cook took her into the cookhouse, the child looked back at the rumpus. The hen had gathered her babies under her wings, cackling loudly, her own hunger forgotten.

The Master's Daughter   Vjange Hazle

The Master's Daughter

The Master's Daughter	Vjange Hazle

CHAPTER 1

The morning sun was bright in the room as fourteen-year-old Felice emerged from her canopied bed, stretching her youthful body while placing her small feet on the polished wooden floor of her bedroom. Across the estate men, women, and children dragged their weary bodies, their workday having begun long before the sun was up. Removing her headscarf, Felice allowed her mass of curls to fall across her shoulders. Discarding her nightgown, she walked across the room to the ancient bureau and picked up her pearl-handled hairbrush.

Grey eyes stared back at her from the smooth plumpness of a round face. Her meaty, pink lips spoke of a mother whose roots were dug deep in Africa and her surprisingly straight nose gave testimony to her European ancestry. Felice brushed the curls that easily sprang back into place. When she was satisfied, she replaced the brush on the bureau. From the wardrobe that stood in a corner of the room, she removed a light cotton dress and pulled it over her head. She brushed her hair again with the same results.

Exiting her room to the landing of the Great House on Greenrock Estate, she listened for a moment to the chatter of the women moving from room to room as they dusted and cleaned.

She was familiar with the lilt of every one of their voices and could recognize them in work song, their hands knocking a rhythm on the coconut brushes they used to keep the floors polished shine. Felice headed down the stairs and across the yard to the cookhouse where Cook was busy, humming a song while she prepared the Massa's breakfast.

"Mornin, Miss Felice," Cook greeted as Felice sank down at the small wooden table near the fireplace where a huge blackened pot rested amidst the leaping flames.

"Cook, how much time I have to tell you to just call me Felice?" she responded, her soft voice attempting a note of authority. "I been coming to you cookhouse since my eye dem at mi knee an helping you…"

"Miss Felice, Massa won't feel too good hearing you talk so bad. After all di learning him been trying to teach you an trying to make you into a lady."

"Chut, Massa can stay. I like come in here an eat your cassava bread an fish…"

"Miss Felice, you going to get me in trouble, you know."

"Don't worry, Cook. I know how to behave when I need to. My father don't have to know."

"You not eating in here one more day, Felice," Cook determined, after pausing a moment to stare at the young girl.

Cook grabbed Felice's hand and half-dragged her out of the cookhouse which smelled of fried plantains, and fish that had not yet been cooked.

"You is a young lady now, Miss Felice and you not like di rest of us. You is Massa own dawta and need to behave dat way all di time."

Felice allowed herself to be led back to the Great House to the breakfast room where an array of fruits was already laid out. Cook glared at her before exiting the room. Felice picked up a ripe mango and sniffed at it. Gone were the days when she would forage for her own fruits in the bushes, climbing the trees with Morgiana, Cook's daughter, and the other children on the estate who were not yet old enough for the gangs.

The day Mr. Henderson had arrived from Scotland four years before was still clear in Felice's mind. Everyone had paused in their work to watch the carriage as it made its way up the hill to come to a stop in front of the Great House. Felice had seen Mr. Henderson only once before when she was about five years old and had really forgotten what he looked like. She had not given much thought to him as the sugar estate went about its business under Mr. Musgrave, the Overseer or Busha.

At age ten, she had watched Henderson's return to Greenrock that would signal a change in her circumstances; a change she had not been prepared for. Hiding behind Cook's skirt, she had taken a peek at the man who sat at the table, his heavy whiskers and eyebrows giving him a formidable appearance.

He was a tall man with thick black hair and piercing blue eyes. Felice could not understand much of what he was saying in his deep, booming voice and Cook had explained that he was from Scotland and that was how they spoke there.

Felice wondered what Scotland was and if everybody there looked like him. He had seen her then and a frown had come across his brow. When Cook had asked her to bring out the tureen of beef stew, she had walked on shaky legs toward the table and its sole occupant, hoping he would not say anything to her to which he expected an answer. Instead, he had glared at her, his frown deepening. He had called Cook to him then and she had heard them whispering in urgent tones. The following day, Felice's life changed.

The small room next to the library that she and Cook and Morgiana shared in the Great House was all Felice knew. The cot in the corner with its sweet, sugary smell was the only bed she could remember. When Cook began packing her things, Felice was curious. But Cook would not answer her when she asked. Cook led her up the stairs of the Great House to one of the rooms she had only seen the inside of a few times and told her this was now her room.

In the center was a large canopied mahogany bed with mosquito nets, a ruffled bed skirt, and an embroidered bedspread. The pillows matching the bedspread were huge and fluffed. Felice felt small as she stared at the bed and wondered how she could sleep all by herself in something so big. There was more than enough room for her, Morgiana, and Cook. The room had a large bureau and mirror, a high chest of drawers, and a wardrobe stood against one wall in one corner. Next to the window was a table with a pitcher and basin. Felice looked up at Cook.

"Listen to me, Felice. Massa Henderson is your father. Him

decide is time you live like a proper lady in the house. Him cannot have you running all ova di place like all dem odda pickney. Behave you self and show him manners. You cannot sleep wid me anymore, you hear?"

Felice stared at Cook. Mr. Henderson her father? How?

"An you cannot come into di cookhouse come help me cook. You is like a Missis now."

Felice's head snapped back.

"How you mean I cyaan come help you cook no more? Me no waan be no Missis."

"Behave you self, chile, an speak proper. Massa Henderson wi talk to you."

Felice felt her panic rise. Mr. Henderson to speak to her?

Aquila, a tall, dark-skinned woman, her head wrapped in a turban, entered the room and Cook made her exit after sending a stern look Felice's way. Aquila looked down at Felice, her look one of utter hatred and disgust.

"No badda tink you betta dan we now, you know."

Felice was not sure what she meant but when the woman began stripping Felice's clothes off her, she panicked.

"A lick you, you see, pickney. Stan steady so mek me wipe you up."

Felice felt self-conscious standing naked in front of this woman who had never shown her a kindness. Roughly, Aquila began scrubbing her with a wet cloth that got dirtier and dirtier. Once she was finished, she went to the wardrobe in which an assortment of clothes hung and pulled out a dress. Walking over to Felice, she grabbed the child's arms, forcing them up while she tugged the dress over her head. She sat Felice down on the stool in front of the bureau and began brushing the child's short hair with a pearl-handled brush. Felice watched the woman's reflection in the mirror. So much hatred she had never seen in her ten years alive.

Cook had always insisted that they keep Felice's hair short because of lice since the child preferred to play in places no one else wanted to. It did not take long for Aquila to complete her task. There had been no gentleness in her touch.

Aquila led Felice to the study where Mr. Henderson sat behind a dark mahogany desk. All around him were books and more books. He glanced up at their entrance. Aquila quickly exited. Felice felt her throat tighten and her knees weaken as he looked her up and down as if assessing something he had purchased.

"What's your name?" he growled at her.

Felice cleared her throat.

"What's a matter? Cat got your tongue?"

"Felice, sah," she whispered hoarsely.

"Felice, huh? Well, Felice, you are a fortunate child. Do you know why you are here?"

"No, Massa," she managed.

"I must provide for my offspring, meaning you. It is only the godly thing to do. From now on you will live as my daughter, though illegitimate. I will see that you are well taken care of. I will provide you with all the clothing and food you need. You will never want. Understand?"

"Yes, Massa."

"God, I must do something about your language. This will not do."

Felice looked down on the floor at her feet encased in a pair of slippers. Her toes and heels she knew were cracked and hardened from planting her feet in the rich soil of the island for most of her ten years. She shifted uncomfortably in the dress.

"And you dinna need to call me Massa."

"Yes, Massa."

"Goddammit!"

Felice flinched.

"Go on, you," he ordered, his tone softening somewhat.

Felice gave a small curtsy and exited the room.

Where must she go now?

Cook did not want her in the cookhouse. She could not go romping with Morgiana and the others in her new clothing and shoes. On top of that, they were all working in the fields at this time of the day, having been up since before sunrise. She had stood outside the door to the study, undecided.

Now, at fourteen, she still was not sure what her place in the household of Mr. Duncan Henderson was.

She never called him Father and never thought of him that way. He was Mr. Henderson, the man from Scotland who every now and then came back to check up on his estate in Jamaica. Felice kept out of his way as much as possible then but she had found herself in Cook's cookhouse more than she should be. After a while, Cook had not seemed to mind her presence and soon she was again accepted at Cook's side, learning to roll the dough while listening to Cook's gossip about everyone working the sugar estate.

Cook was the only cook on the estate even though she had a girl to assist her. Her job was to provide meals for the Overseer or Busha and the Bookkeeper when Mr. Henderson was away. Mr. Henderson himself did not ask for any special provisions while he was there but Cook went all out anyway for her master when he did come. Morning, noon, and evening she cooked and lay out a spread. Felice was always at her elbow handing her something or trying to help knead the flour and, even though Cook kept reminding her that she really should not be there, she never told her to leave.

Until now when she was bodily dragged from the cookhouse and deposited in the breakfast room.

Felice bit into her mango, skin and all, taking care not to let the juice drip onto her dress. There were knives and spoons but she still felt awkward using them to eat the fruit. It was much more delicious tearing the pulp from the seed and feeling the juice slide down to her elbows. She liked to tear a hole in the top of the mango and suck out the flesh until the skin clung to the seed. She didn't care if the worms had got it.

After four years of living in the Great House she still was not used to the life. Immediately after ensconcing her in the house four years earlier, her father had gone off to the capital and then on to Scotland. She had not seen him since and somewhat hoped that he was gone for good.

Until yesterday.

Duncan Henderson's arrival the day before had been unforeseen. Accompanying him was a whole house-full of new furniture and furnishings. Felice was unsure of what was happening. Cook would not tell her anything and she was afraid to ask Mr. Henderson. Cook entered the dining room with her breakfast and Felice sat down at the table. The steam rose from the bowl of porridge and plate of cassava bread and fish that were placed in front of her.

"This look good, Cook," she observed as she picked up her spoon.

"Say your grace before you eat," Cook reminded with a firm

gentleness.

"Yes, ma'am," Felice teased but dutifully closed her eyes and muttered a quick prayer like Cook had taught her.

The house was all a-flurry as the housemaids cleaned and changed drapes and furniture was re-arranged. Felice watched and wondered what was going on but no one would breathe a word to her.

It was funny how the people she had known all of her fourteen years suddenly became different people the moment she had moved fully into the house. Aquila had openly displayed her hatred for her and her new status while the others barely spoke to her. The children she had romped with, stoning trees and bathing in the river were suddenly calling her names like 'Red-Ibo' and 'Malatta' and had seemed afraid to draw her into their company. The only friend she seemed to have been able to keep was Cook's daughter Morgiana. She missed nights talking with Morgie, even though most of the time the girl was too tired from working to talk much.

Felice finished her breakfast without encountering her father. She hoped she did not run into him at all. She wandered into the cookhouse again where Cook was starting to wash up so she could begin to prepare lunch. It was tempting to roll her sleeves up and help the only woman who had paid her any attention without displaying any animosity. But she did not want her hands slapped at the moment.

"What you doing in here?" Cook demanded.

"Nothing."

"Devil find work fi idle hands."

Apart from helping Cook in the cookhouse, Felice had never really worked on the estate. When Morgiana was sent to the cane field, she had wanted to go too. But, Cook had told her no. Her place was with her. But she had had to beg Cook to show her what to do. There was nothing in particular that she had been assigned to. She would have gladly dusted the furniture like Queen and the other women did. Or shine the floor with the brush made from the coconut like Essie and her group of house servants did. She had not thought about that before, but now she understood her special position as the daughter of the estate owner.

She sat at the cookhouse table and watched Cook scrub the pots with the coconut husk and ash from the fireside, her fleshy arms covered black up to her elbows.

"Cook, what is going on?"

"Why you asking me?"

"Because nobody else won't tell me."

"Doan worry you self. Just make sure you show manners and dat will carry you through."

"Mr. Henderson go married?"

"Hah."

"How come everybody hiding tings from me?"

"Felice, stop boddering me. I have work fi do."

"I going ask Morgie."

"You leave Morgiana alone. She have work to do. You will find out soon enough what going on. Miss Clementine coming today?"

"Yes."

"Make sure you take the learnings. Is not everyday somebody like you get a chance fi learn book. Take it, Miss Felice, while you can. It will serve you in a time of need."

"What you mean by dat, Cook?"

"Just listen to what me say. Your father not going to be alive all di time to make sure you alright. Take book, for one day you might have to go out into di world on yuh own."

"What you talkin about?"

A high-pitched female voice interrupted their conversation, calling out her name, and Felice dashed off the stool and headed for the study, being careful to walk as she approached the room. A slender white woman of about thirty was standing at the door to the study. She was wearing a long white cotton frock that belted at the waist with a satin ribbon. Underneath the dress, she wore a petticoat, and on her head a ribbon hat which had a freshly picked hibiscus stuck in the band.

Clementine Rutherfurd was an attractive woman who had made her way on the *Jamaica Packet* from Edinburgh to the island three years before, accompanied by her brother. There was rampant speculation about what would make an attractive, spinster woman undertake such a journey and decide to stay on an island that offered her no prospects. Rumors were flying all around the island to which Felice was not yet privy and which seemed to not have reached Duncan Henderson's ears. This was, after all, one of the tropical colonies where the heat did not come from just the sun and where the blood of its inhabitants seemed to boil to overflow with passions unspoken.

The European men in the colonies seemed to prefer the company of the slave women who inhabited the estates and plantations. Miss Rutherfurd had ceased being shocked each time she came across a fair-skinned child who was somewhere in between. Mixed race children seemed to now be the rule for those who decided to make this their home, the fathers often sending these children to Europe for their education. A white woman on the island was as welcome as a cankerous sore on the foot. Felice curtsied in front of the woman.

"Good morning, Miss Rutherfurd," she greeted in an affected tone.

"Good morning, Felice. Are you ready for the day's activities?"

"Most certainly, ma'am," Felice answered and preceded her into the room, resigning herself to a morning of learning.

The morning went by quickly as Felice made a pretense of being a diligent student. Every now and then she gazed longingly out the window, especially when she heard someone's call, a voice she recognized. She longed to be running around with Morgiana. But, Cook had told her those days were over. Those she had grown up with were now in the fields from morning to night. She was now a young lady and needed to conduct herself as one.

Felice remembered the morning when she was about twelve and had awakened to find her sheets bloodied; she did not know what to do. When Aquila came in to fill her basin with fresh water, she had screamed at her and called her nasty. After much reassurance that Felice had not let in one of the boys from the estate in the middle of the night, Aquila had made some kind of padding for her by folding cloths, which she kept secured by tying a string around Felice's waist. Felice had made her way to the cookhouse, afraid to walk too fast in case the padding fell from between her legs. Cook asked her why she was walking like that. When she explained, Cook looked at her, trying to suppress a smile. Then she told her what it meant including the warning to stay clear of the men on the estate.

Each morning Felice received her education in decorum and learned to read and write. She often wondered why Miss Rutherfurd did not seem to observe the decorum she taught as the woman removed her hat and loosened her bodice the moment the door to the study closed behind them.

She blamed the excessive heat and fanned herself continually.

While Felice read, Miss Rutherfurd pulled out a book from her case. Felice struggled to catch a glance at the title. But, Miss Rutherfurd's grey eyes bored into hers. Felice determined to discover what Miss Rutherfurd read that made her so hot and bothered.

The Master's Daughter   Vjange Hazle

CHAPTER 2

The carriage rumbled up the hill and came to a stop in front of the Great House. Felice peeked from behind the heavy drapes in the drawing room and watched the occupants alight. It had been a busy morning as the final touches were put on the house to welcome the new occupants. The house was like new; even the yard seemed to have been washed clean. The slaves in the field paused a moment to watch the cloud of dust that signaled their arrival, risking the wrath of the Driver.

The woman who alighted was long-faced with a nose that seemed to have spent its entire thirty years pointed in the air. Her dark green gown was heavy and unsuited for the tropical climate. Her blond hair was partially hidden by a hat studded with what looked like flowers. Beneath this, rivulets of sweat were dripping down the sides of her face and onto her dress. She stood for a moment in the open carriage surveying everything around her before turning to the two children who gazed in wonder at the house and vast fields below and around them. The footmen alighted, one extending his hand to the new lady of the house. Mary Henderson paused a moment before lightly resting a gloved hand in that of the Negro to her right.

Duncan Henderson came around from the other side of the carriage to take his wife's arm.

The butler Lincoln, Cook, Abba the Laundress, and the other house slaves stood in line, waiting for their inspection by their new Missis. Mary Henderson barely glanced at them as she made her way up the steps of the Great House. The children followed behind their parents, marveling at the two-storied house with its wrap-around verandah and high windows on the first floor and balconies on the second.

"You mean this is all ours, Father?" five year old Duncan II questioned in wonder.

"I'm afraid so, lad," his father responded with a chuckle. "Come along, Rebecca."

The children followed their parents into the hallway from which a single flight of stairs led to the second floor landing. Felice watched from her hiding place in the drawing room as the new arrivals surveyed their surroundings. Then, in a moment of panic, she realized that they were heading in her direction. What must she do? She did not want to be seen. Quickly, she dashed through the side door of the drawing room to the verandah.

"What was that?" Mary Henderson asked as she headed for the camel-backed sofa, pulling the hat off her head as she lowered herself onto the seat.

"Must be one of the servants," her husband responded, entering behind her.

Cook entered the room with a tray of glasses and beverage followed by the girl Nancy with a tray of biscuits and fruit.

Mrs. Henderson stared at them, unused to being served by women of their kind who appeared dusty and unwashed.

"This will certainly take some getting used to," she exclaimed as she took the proffered drink in which slices of lemon floated.

"Indeed, mother," eight-year-old Rebecca agreed. "They are so…well…hideously black."

"Come, come, Becca," her father reprimanded. "They might be slaves but there is no cause to be rude."

"Do they even understand when we speak, father?" young Duncan queried.

"That will be enough of that. Cook, where has Felice gone to?"

"You need her, Massa?"

"No, no. Just thought she would have been about. No matter. Baths need to be drawn for the Missis. Let Adolphus and Felix know."

Cook curtsied and left after a wicked glance at the new family. She found Felice in the cookhouse.

"Massa been asking for you."

"Why?"

"How I must know? All I know is di devil wife herself just walk into dat house."

"What you mean, Cook?"

"Hmmm" Cook groaned deeply. "Mark my word."

Felice ignored Cook and sat watching her. The woman was dragging pots and pans, her lips set in a tight line. Cook was definitely not pleased with her new responsibilities.

Felice was not sure how she herself felt about this woman and her two children. Was she now to call her mother and the children brother and sister? It was strange to her that these two children from another place could call her sister.

Dinner was served at six in the evening and Felice was commanded by her father to be there and on time. Felice stared at her reflection in the looking-glass as she got ready to go down the stairs. She would have been glad to eat in the cookhouse with Cook, instead of facing these strangers who were somehow her family. She surveyed her features, wondering who the woman who had given birth to her was. She knew it was not Mary Henderson. She had once asked Cook who her mother was and the response was that she did not need to worry about it. Felice's fingers traced their path along the contours of her face. Who was the woman who had given her the thick lips and dark tinted skin that set her apart from most of the others on the estate?

She heard her name being called and she hurried downstairs to the dining room. The family was already seated and Felice took one of the empty chairs at the table across from the children.

Mrs. Henderson had changed into a simple blue gown that, while still unsuited for the tropics, was much lighter than the one in which she had arrived. Her hair was now piled on top of her head and twisted into a neat bun. Her skin was somewhat flushed at the unaccustomed heat. Rebecca sat next to her brother in a yellow frock under which she was not wearing a petticoat. Her brother wore a simple white shirt and trousers.

"What is *she* doing here?" Mrs. Henderson asked from her position opposite her husband, her thin face drawn thinner as she looked haughtily down her nose at the girl sitting at her dining table across from her son and daughter.

"Felice stays," her husband countered.

"But, she is a Negro. She belongs outside."

"Mulatto," her husband corrected, "and she stays."

"Why must she?"

"Because, my dear wife, Felice happens to be my daughter."

Mary Henderson's knife and fork clattered to the plate. The children stared at their father who was busily cutting his beef into chewable pieces. Mrs. Henderson strove to retain her composure.

"What? But h-how?"

"A liaison in my youth, my dear. As you can see it involved one in my employ."

Mary Henderson was silent. Slowly she placed the napkin on the table and rose. She looked disgustedly at Felice.

"How could you?"

"That was before your time, Mary, dear. Nothing to fuss about."

"Nothing to fuss about? Nothing to fuss about?" her voice was rising to a frenzied pitch.

"Is she then our sister, Father?" Rebecca asked.

"Never!" her mother screamed as she ran from the table and swiftly exited the room.

Duncan Henderson placed pieces of meat into his mouth as if he had only just informed her that the weather could change from sunshine to thunderous dark in moments on this tropical island. His children stared at him. Rebecca made a move to follow her mother.

"Sit!" her father commanded, still focused on his meal.

The children eyed Felice suspiciously as the girl stared at her empty plate. Felice could feel the accusations coming from across the table. She wanted to ask for the tureen to be passed to her so she could have her share of Cook's beef stew with a touch of molasses. She wanted to ask for a glass of Beveridge to soothe her throat that had gone dry. She wanted to look up and smile into the faces of the children who called her father 'Father'. Cook entered followed by Nancy.

"Everyting alright, Massa?" she asked, glancing at the top of Felice's head.

"Yes, yes. The Missis is not feeling too well at the moment. Too much heat. She will soon be alright."

"Felice not eating?"

"A bit shy, I'm afraid. Fill her plate, will you, Isabella?"

Dutifully Cook spooned beef stew onto the girl's plate along with potatoes and bananas. She stood next to the girl, hoping she would glance up.

"Miss Felice, it not going get any better. Eat. You need your strength to fight any ting dat comes your way, even the devil wife herself," Cook commanded gently, her eyes on Henderson.

Felice paused. She tried to quell the pain in her heart at the rejection. If this was what the future held for her then she would just go back to her little room with Cook and Morgiana. She would even learn to work in the cane fields if she had to. Dusting the furniture in the Great House was not a bad thing. It was better than learning the books and trying to act and speak like the lady Miss Rutherfurd was trying to make her into. Where was she going to go anyway where she needed to act like a lady? Yes, she would ask Cook to assign her duties in the house.

"Father..." Rebecca ventured.

"Eat," her father responded as he continued eating. "Felice, you will eat."

Felice picked up her knife and fork and slowly cut her food, head still bent.

"Dat how Miss Clementine learn you to sit, Miss Felice?" Cook asked softly.

Felice straightened. Cook patted her on the shoulder before stepping back and exiting the dining room, Nancy in tow.

The silence hung heavy in the room. Felice fixed her eyes somewhere above the heads of the children and tried to finish her meal, wondering how she was going to live in this house with a woman and her children who hated her so for no reason.

At rooster crow the following morning, Felice awoke to the sound of the opening of her room door. Aquila entered with a pitcher of water and poured the liquid into the basin under the window. Felice washed her face and changed into the dress Aquila handed her.

"Tank God I don't have to look afta di likes of you anymore," Aquila volunteered.

"What do you mean by that, Aquila?"

"I get to be Missis maid now. She might make you maid too. Heh-heh. How di mighty have fallen."

"But I am Massa daughter."

"Dastard. You did tink is all di day of your life you was gwine lie down all day like a Missis? Now real Missis come so step back, you old Malatta crosses," Aquila declared, pointing a finger in Felice's face.

Felice was silent. Could Mrs. Henderson do that? She was the Master's daughter. No one had made her work all these years. Could Mrs. Henderson now make her into a maid? Maybe that would be better than having to sit at a table where she was not wanted. She finished dressing after Aquila sauntered out of the room, unsure whether to go downstairs to the breakfast room where she might meet Mary Henderson. She must find Cook.

She could hear Cook's voice raised in a quarrel as she entered the cooking house. Nancy stood in a corner almost shivering as the older woman seemed to tower over her. Felice could not remember hearing Cook quarrel with anyone except maybe the yard boy who had tried to sell her a meager string of fish for more than it was worth. He had never tried doing that again. Or Long Dick who had tried to sell her young yam. Cook had accused him of trying to kill her and the Massa.

"What is going on here?" Felice asked.

"None of your business. What you doing here?" Cook responded without turning around.

"I..."

"Miss Felice, go to the house so have your breakfast before it cold and stop boddering me."

Felice hesitated.

"Gwaan," Cook commanded.

Felice felt the tears coming as she turned away. Then Cook was upon her, fleshy arms engulfing her, dragging her to her bosom.

"Sorry, Miss Felice. I never mean to talk to you like dat. I forget miself. Please forgive me."

The scent of seasonings meant to stifle her as Felice's face was pressed into Cook's ample bosom. The woman cooed and begged for forgiveness as one hand stroked Felice's hair. Felice struggled for her breath and finally escaped.

"I just doan like to see anybody take disadvantage of anyone. Miss Felice, you mustn't mek dat devil woman mek you fraid, you hear? Walk wid you head high. You is you fadda dawta. Doan forget. No mek she feel like she can beat you down."

Felice sniffled, recalling those same arms holding her close at night, body smelling of powder, so different from the smells of her trade that now emanated from her. Whether she had a fever or was afraid because of the whipping rains and wind that were threatening to bring the Great House down, Cook's arms were always her place to run to. She and Morgie would climb into Cook's narrow bed and under her arms where they would fall asleep in their place of comfort.

"Come, go eat before Massa start call fi you," Cook advised as she pushed Felice from her. "Remember what me tell you."

Felice hurried off to the Great House. Her father was seated at the table and so were the two children. Mrs. Henderson had chosen to have her coffee and breakfast on the upper balcony of her room. Felice bid good morning and sat. The children watched her suspiciously as they spooned their porridge into their mouths. Their father was taking them for a tour of the plantation, he advised. Felice was to carry on as usual with Miss Rutherfurd and have her lessons.

But Felice could not focus on her lessons as she fretted on what her future would be with Mrs. Henderson as mistress. She had not seen the woman all day, even when the children returned from their tour, hot and dusty as they fanned themselves and begged for something cool to drink. Rebecca's hair was falling out of its clasp, hanging in wisps around her head and young Duncan was panting as if he was a puppy out in the sun too long.

"It is infernally hot," Rebecca commented, flopping down on the settee in the drawing room.

"Watch your language, young lady," her father cautioned as he hung his hat.

Felice rose from her seat where she had been trying to read the book assigned her by Miss Rutherfurd. Mrs. Henderson suddenly appeared, looking down her nose at her own dusty children. Her gown was laced to her throat and the long sleeves hid her arms. Sweat glistened on her brow.

"Really, Duncan, must you take them traipsing through this

infernal jungle? Look at them. Becca with no hat on. Soon she will be as black as these savages. And what is *she* doing sitting here as if she is Missis? I will not have this, Duncan. I most certainly will not."

"Children, run off to Aquila and get cleaned up."

"Which one is Aquila?" Rebecca queried innocently. "They all look the same to me."

"Call her name and she will answer," their father suggested.

The children ran off and Duncan Henderson turned to face his wife. Felice sat uncertainly, her book clasped in her hand. Henderson towered over his wife and Felice shivered a little. She had never really seen him angry.

"Felice is my child," he grated. "She has every right to be here. She was here before you came and will be here long after you have gone. You will either love it or leave it, understood?"

His wife stared at him for a moment. She then glanced at Felice before wheeling from the room. Henderson turned to face Felice. He gave her a wan smile before leaving the room.

Felice stood in the middle of the drawing room, undecided where she should go. It seemed everywhere she went no one wanted her there, from Cook to the other servants to Henderson and his family.

CHAPTER 3

The dinner guests marveled at the fare, complimenting the cook and her staff. Cook had pulled in six women and a man to help prepare the feast for the evening with twenty guests and the family of five. She had bossed them like a true slave master should until they did what she asked of them. She smiled broadly as she watched the party devour the meal with delight.

Felice sat across the table from her half brother and sister. Their eyes were wide with amazement at the motley crew in various styles of dress seated around the long dining table. Her father was seated at the head of the table and his wife a distant opposite end, her face a dark mask.

Their nearest neighbor Mr. McDowell tore at his leg of chicken from where he sat opposite Felice. He was an Englishman who looked like he should be a gentleman but rumors had it otherwise. His nails gave signs that he worked the earth himself. His son Mulatto John sat next to Felice.

Mulatto John was a golden haired boy of the same age as Felice. His mother, Felice heard, was the slave wife of McDowell. Could she and John be brother and sister, Felice wondered? Could the woman who had given birth to John have also birthed her?

Maybe she could ask Cook although it was not the first time she had tried to get information from the woman about her mother. Cook had always sent her away or pretended she did not know what Felice was talking about.

John was silent as he ate and Felice could see he was not at ease from the shaking of his hands as he held his knife and fork. Someone must have shown him how to use the utensils. He held them well but he was ill at ease with them. His nails were much cleaner than his father's as if someone had taken care to make him presentable. He wore a waistcoat and a shirt that looked like it had belonged to someone else who was much bigger; perhaps something handed down from his father. He had a dusty smell but Felice did not find it repellant.

How she wished he would talk to her. Everyone else at the table, apart from Mary Henderson, seemed engaged in conversation. Miss Rutherfurd seemed determined to make McDowell's acquaintance with her bosom overflowing the neckline of her white cotton dress.

McDowell owned a large estate a few miles distant and was considered successful if not somewhat wealthy; but his reputation was known throughout the island. He was a man who took his pleasures wherever and whenever he wanted. His preference was for the women whose dark skins proclaimed their rights to being nonexistent. He felled them where he found them: in the fields, along the roadside, and anywhere else it was convenient for him to mount them. Miss

Rutherfurd did not stand a chance in her white skin and plumped bodice. But, she did not know that.

Dinner ended, the party retired to the drawing room where the chatter continued. Mary Henderson excused herself, proclaiming the tropical heat had got to her. She took her offspring with her.

Felice sat on an armchair and was surprised to see Mulatto John take the chair next to her. Maybe he was feeling just as left out as she was, noting that there was no one else like himself at the party.

"How many years are you?" Felice ventured.

He cleared his throat before responding.

"I am fourteen years."

His voice sounded almost like a man's with a bit if a crackle.

"I am fourteen years too," Felice returned with a note of delight in her voice.

So, this would mean they could not be brother and sister.

"Mr. Henderson is your father then?" he asked.

"Yes, but I don't know who my mother is."

"My mother Abigail is a free woman but she cannot be here. She is a Negro, though very light-skinned."

Felice wondered if her mother was a Negro too. It must be. Her father was a white man. Maybe her mother was a slave on another plantation. But then, that would make her a slave too. How could that be when she was free and able to roam the plantation as she wished? Had her own father freed her?

"Do you ride?" John was asking.

"No."

"My father gave me a horse. I named him Brutus. I could teach you to ride him."

Felice's heart leaped. She was not sure how she felt about horses. She had seen them at a distance and they looked taller than the tallest man. They were always snorting like they wanted to fight and stomped restlessly.

"You don't need to be afraid of Brutus," he continued. "He is gentle. Besides, I will help you."

"Alright," Felice finally agreed.

"I will meet you by the river tonight so we won't be seen. I will whistle twice and wait by the tamarind tree. I often go riding at night."

"Why at night?"

"The night covers you. No one can tell who you are then. You could be Backra Massa himself for all they know."

Felice thought of the darkness of the night with its croaking toads and creatures that called from the bushes. She had never ventured forth beyond the setting of the sun. Cook had warned her of the other creatures who loved the night. There was the three-foot horse and the rolling calf whose eyes were red as fire and who roamed the land dragging his chain. The old woman who flew in a ball of fire at night, the *soucouyant*, searching for someone whose blood she could suck, was the one she was most afraid of.

As Mulatto John smiled at her, Felice felt a reassurance that she would be safe. His light brown eyes danced in his face. His cheeks still rosy from boyhood were showing signs of downy hair that would become whiskers someday. And his lips, curved into a smile, held a promise of something. She did not know what.

"Come on, boy," McDowell called to his son.

John smiled his goodbye as he rose. Felice felt her heart flip. It was so good to find a friend. For too long she had been the one left out. Now she had found one like herself.

Later that night when all was quiet in the Great House, Felice was about. Tiptoeing barefooted down the stairs to Cook's room, she felt like a girl on a mission.

Ever since she had talked with Mulatto John, she had a nagging inside of her to find out who her mother was and was determined to find out tonight or she could not sleep.

The door opened easily and without a sound.

She could make out Morgiana's form wrapped in her thin sheet. The girl fell asleep easily after a long day of working the cane fields in the broiling sun and could not be awakened until the first cock-crow. Often she would not even change into her nightclothes but slept as she came in. Felice wished she could sometimes make it easier for her friend and childhood companion. But it was the way of the estate and Morgiana was only one of those suffering such a fate, a curse of their dark skin.

Felice hated waking Cook but she just must know tonight. As she reached for the human bulk on Cook's bed to shake her awake, she became aware that something was amiss.

Cook lay sprawled on her back, her nightdress pulled up to her neck and there was someone atop her. As her eyes became accustomed to the darkness, Felice's eyes connected first with Cook's wide ones and then those of her father whose white buttocks were outlined by the pale moonlight streaming through the window.

Cook raised a finger to her lips as if to say 'hush'. But a gasp had already escaped Felice's lips. Morgiana grumbled but did not awaken. Felice stared from one to the other and then she slowly backed out the way she had come in.

Dashing out the front door of the Great House, she ran down the hill toward the river, her nightdress billowing in the wind, the grass cool beneath her feet. She tried not to think of what she had just seen as her eyes searched the darkness for Mulatto John. She heard a whistle. He had been waiting.

The shape of a horse loomed in the darkness and the animal snorted. The figure of a man detached itself from the trunk of the tamarind tree and Felice recognized Mulatto John. Silently he held her hand and led her to the horse.

The animal was as black as the night as it swished its tail and Felice could swear its eyes blazed with fire. John patted the horse's side before taking Felice's hand in his and running it down its body. He cooed softly to the horse, all the while holding Felice's hand so she could feel the animal too. He leaped onto the horse's back and reached down a hand to her. Placing a bare foot onto his booted one, she allowed him to pull her up alongside him. He seated her before him. Felice felt herself tremble a bit in the cool night air and the unaccustomed feel of an animal beneath her. And a male body so close to hers.

Slowly, John guided the horse along the banks of the river, all the while a hand across Felice's waist to hold her secure. She tried to not worry too much sitting high above the ground and the branches of the trees so close to her head. John's arm held her safe. They rode in silence, listening to the night and each other's breathing.

Felice started when she heard the hoot of a *Patoo*. People said someone was going to die when you heard a *Patoo*.

A chill ran through her. John tightened his hold on her ever so slightly. They did not ride for long and they returned to the tamarind tree where he helped her down and slid off to stand in front of her. Felice hurried off, aware of his shadow watching and waiting until she disappeared from view.

Then she heard his horse's hooves as he pounded off toward his home.

Felice awoke the following morning to a soreness she had never before experienced. The night before felt like part of her dream. She was still riding, John's arm securing her. Suddenly the horse shied, throwing her off. But, it was John who was falling, disappearing into darkness as she tried to reach him to bring him back. Felice awakened with a start and memories came flooding back to her.

She wasn't sure how to face Cook knowing what she had seen the night before. She was young but was not completely innocent to what a man and woman did to each other. Too many times she and Morgie had encountered a couple who had snuck off from work for a moment in the cane field or behind a bush or tree. Sometimes following a giggle would lead them to hitched up skirt and dropped trousers. But Cook? And her father?

Felice no longer had her own maid; but she did not care. It had been awkward to have someone come in and dress her when she could do it herself. She cleaned herself using water from the pitcher under the window and hurriedly put on a light cotton dress. Today she wished she had someone to help her dress. The soreness extended all over her body.

She made her way down the stairs to her old haunt: Cook's cookhouse. The woman glanced at her as she entered.

"Mornin, Miss Felice," she greeted in a low tone, returning to her task of rolling flour between her palms and dropping them into the lard.

"Morning, Cook," Felice returned.

There was silence. Normally Cook would begin a tirade and send her off to find something to do. Felice had never seen her subdued. She sat silently at the cookhouse table.

"What you want, Miss Felice?" Cook finally asked.

"Nothing. I just came to see if you need my help."

Cook gave a short chuckle.

"You know better dan dat, Miss Felice."

"Cook, may I ask you a question?"

The woman's hand hovered with a ball of flour, poised to deposit in the pan.

"Who is my mother?"

Cook placed the ball into the pan, using her hand to turn the others as they browned. The smell of frying flour teased Felice's nostrils and made her stomach growl.

"Me."

Felice was unsure she had heard the woman.

"What?"

"You hear me, Miss Felice. Don't go on like you hard a hearing now. I am you modda. Missa Henderson is you fadda."

Felice mouth stood agape. How could that be? How could Cook be her mother? The events of the night before came back to her along with memories of other times she had awakened to someone else in the room she had shared with Cook and Morgiana. Morgiana. She was her sister. Morgie was her sister.

"Why you never tell me before?"

"It never matter. Why it matter now? Can't change anyting."

Felice felt a bit of anger at the woman who, for fourteen years had hidden from her the most important thing about herself. Cook had been nothing but good to her, she had to admit. But to not tell her that she was the woman who had given birth to her, even after she had asked so many times. Why would she admit it now?

"Don't expect me to call you mama," Felice finally said as she walked out of the room back to the Great House.

As Felice entered the verandah, she encountered Mary Henderson who seemed to have been waiting for her.

The woman was more sensibly dressed in a long cotton gown whose neckline was more accommodating of the heat. Her hair was piled on top of her head. She looked down the length of her nose at Felice.

"Can you read?" the woman queried harshly.

"Yes," Felice responded, her hands folded on each other in front of her.

This was the first time since her arrival that the woman had addressed her directly.

"You will address me as Missis. Can you read?"

"Yes, Missis."

"You will then be assigned to young Duncan and Rebecca. You will see to their needs."

"Yes, Missis."

"Let it be understood that, no matter the circumstance, you are not brother and sister. You will treat them as your master and mistress. You will never, *never*, be their equal."

The last words were ground out between her teeth and her eyes bulged threateningly in her head. In that moment, Felice knew what the old hag, the *soucouyant* looked like.

"Yes, Missis."

Felice hurried to her room.

So, finally Mary Henderson had made her a maid. Aquila had said it would happen. Her brother and sister were to be her master and mistress.

She was the daughter of a slave so what could she expect?

Felice had not had time to think about Cook's revelation earlier that morning. *All this time.* All this time she had been living with her own mother at hand and she did not know. How could Cook do this to her? The woman was nothing but good to her but still, to keep such a secret was something she could not think to forgive.

A knock came at her door and Felice rose to open to Aquila who stood as haughty as her Missis.

"Miss Mary want you to come to the children room," Aquila declared with as much Europeanness as she had learned since her advancement.

Rising, Felice followed Aquila down the hall to the suite of rooms she knew the children occupied.

The rooms were joined by a sitting area in which the children now sat expectantly on a small settee. Their mother stood above them, refusing to look directly at Felice after the initial glance.

"You will be here as soon as the children awaken to dress them and see to their studies. You will accompany them to their meals and take them for walks before the sun goes down. You will put them to bed at night. Understood?"

"Yes, Missis."

A snicker came from somewhere behind Felice and she knew it must have come from Aquila.

"If I ever get a report from them, you will be dismissed from the estate forthwith. You complain to Mr. Henderson and I will make your existence even more miserable than it is now, you wretched bastard."

Felice winced before accepting her assignment with a curtsy. Mary Henderson wheeled out of the room, Aquila at her heels imitating her mistress' stance. The children sat staring up at Felice.

Before Felice could approach the two, someone breezed into the room. Cook stood in the middle of the room, her chest heaving.

"Is true?" the woman asked, her arms akimbo.

"Yes," Felice responded, looking shamefaced.

Felice felt the grasp of her mother's hand as she dragged her from the room. A distant memory stirred of a time Cook had rescued her from a fowl that was rushing toward her. Felice glanced around at the astonished faces of the two children, Rebecca rising as if she was ready for a fight.

Cook dragged Felice to the study where Duncan Henderson was immersed in going over the books with his bookkeeper.

"Mista Henderson," Cook addressed the man as he paused to look up at her. "Dis cannot work."

"What the devil is this all about now, Isabella?"

"She turn Felice into a maid," Cook explained, her chest heaving.

"Whatever are you talking about, woman? Who did what?"

"Miss Mary make Felice the children them maid. What you going to do about dat?"

Henderson glanced at the bookkeeper who was sitting across from him. The man unfolded his thin, long frame and exited the room quietly.

"Now, Isabella, I won't have you barging in like this when I am in the middle of work," Henderson scolded, a note of softness to his voice. "It is just not done."

Cook stared at him in silence. Felice fidgeted. She had never seen anything like this.

"I will speak with Mrs. Henderson," he promised, looking back down at the open book.

Cook remained standing before him, her grasp on Felice's arm slackened but her stance still demanding redress.

"Oh, bloody hell. I will speak with her as soon as you leave."

Cook did not move. Henderson uttered a curse and rose. As he left the room, a small smile tugged at the corners of Cook's mouth. Felice stood, dumbfounded.

"Now, dat's how you deal wid a man," she counseled as she exited the room, Felice shuffling behind her.

That night Felice awaited Mulatto John but he did not appear. She wanted to tell him all that had happened to her since they had last been together. A fortnight passed and he still did not come and Felice returned to her everyday life on the estate. Only now, she had to endure the darts of hate from Mary Henderson.

Duncan Henderson told his wife in no uncertain terms that Felice was off limits to her. Felice was his daughter, his flesh and blood. Whatever the law said it did not matter. In his eyes, she was free and he was providing for her. If she, Mary, did not like that then she could bloody well return to Scotland. He was ready to book her passage.

Felice listened quietly as she stood below the balcony of Mary Henderson's quarters. She had not meant to listen but her attention was caught by the raised voices. Mary Henderson sobbed softly and Felice almost felt sorry for her. Her pity disappeared the next time she encountered the woman and she all but spat at Felice.

The children avoided Felice like they heard she had Yaws.

The rainy season was at its end and Mary Henderson seemed to be adjusting to the tropics in her own fashion. Maybe because she spent most of her days on the verandah of her quarters calling out to the servants to attend to her needs.

She called for coffee to be brought to her bedside at daybreak and breakfasted alone as she surveyed the estate from her perch. At noon, she was served her luncheon and by six, she had her dinner brought to her. All throughout the day, the servants fanned her against the tropical heat while she sipped on Beveridge.

She hired a governess, a mulatto creole woman who had been sent to England by her landowning father to be educated. Upon returning to the island, Teresa Duglass took up residence in a room adjoining the children's quarters as tutor and governess to the Henderson children.

One morning young Duncan reported to his governess that he was feeling unwell. Teresa Duglass touched a hand to his forehead.

"My, you are burning up, young one," she affected, the creole drawl barely evident in her speech.

Doctor Bayly was called and it was determined that the child had the Yellow Fever and had to be confined to bed. Mary Henderson hovered over her child, a slight plumpness to her once slender frame.

The following day Rebecca would not eat and complained that her head and back hurt. Doctor Bayly returned.

For four days Mary Henderson sat by her children's beds, wringing her hands and cursing the dark place she had followed her husband to. She forced them to drink the broth Cook prepared using chicken innards and feet. She mopped their brows and wiped their little bodies down with cool water Aquila brought in a basin. And she prayed for their recovery, promising God that if he spared her children, she would leave this God-forsaken land and return to her beloved home, the blessed place where darkness was used only to describe the night.

How could this be when the cursed child of her husband's lust walked about, her bosom blossoming to become a woman's, her complexion robust and healthy as she walked about the plantation as if she truly owned it? Felice must go, Mary Henderson decided while she prayed, her heart full at the disgrace her husband had brought to her.

Young Duncan and his sister Rebecca slowly returned to health. Mary Henderson stayed, biding her time until they were fully recovered and could travel. Her husband was not privy to her plans as she made discreet inquiries as to how she could book their passage as quietly and as quickly as possible.

"My children remain here with me," Duncan Henderson bellowed when news reached him of his wife's plans.

Mary Henderson sobbed where she sat in the shadows on her verandah.

She should have known that the mulatto Teresa Duglass could not be trusted. How could she have thought to confide in that abomination, a creole who could not even speak without her native drawl coming through? But, since arriving on the island, Mary had not made any friends and the closest was the creole woman who tutored her children. Her color was so high she could almost pass for a white person.

Never, Mary swore, even as she spoke to the woman of her plans in muted tones, thankful to find someone with some English education who did not simply grunt responses or complain about the heat in that infernal drawl so typical of the creoles on the island.

So Mary Henderson confined herself to her quarters, eating and imbibing spirits and soon became unrecognizable as the woman who had not long ago arrived to rule her husband's domain.

Felice felt sorry for her but could not understand why the woman wanted to leave a place where she was missis and did not have to work the fields under the hot broiling sun like the dark skinned who became only darker and more angry under the brutal sun and the Massa's whip. She did not have to rid herself of ticks at the end of the day or remove jiggers from her foot like the workers who walked barefooted and barely clothed through the cane fields. There was no one to whip her until she was senseless if she slowed in her step; or *cum* her in the field before throwing a few bits her way. Mary Henderson would never be a slave.

CHAPTER 4

"The American colonies have finally declared their independence, it seems," Duncan Henderson was saying as he chewed on his beef.

"About time," McDowell responded, his knife slicing through the chunk of yellow yam on his plate. "God knows we've suffered enough with all the trade restrictions."

"They are about to ship those Loyalists to the colony too, I hear," Henderson continued. "Like *we* don't have enough troubles already. What with trying to feed our own slaves, they're bringing their own."

The conversation flowed over Felice's head as she sat trying to eat the food set before her. Her eyes kept straying to the figure of a man sitting next to McDowell. It had been two years since she had seen him. Mulatto John. Felice's stomach fluttered as his eyes connected with hers. He smiled and she quickly looked down at her plate.

She was anxious to discover what had happened with him all this time. Why had he stayed away? Had she done something wrong to make him want to not go riding with her again? Maybe his father had discovered that they had gone riding together and stopped him from coming to the estate.

His face had lost most of its softness and had become strongly sculpted like a man's. He had grown whiskers which he kept neatly trimmed along with a small moustache. And he was handsome unlike any man she had ever seen with that small smile curving the corners of his mouth. Felice felt her body growing warm. She must eat but her stomach would not let her.

The dinner seemed a long one with her father, McDowell, and a Mr. Long conversing on matters she did not care about. More rumors of the slaves planning revolts. Young Duncan and his sister Rebecca, now fully recovered and seemingly healthy, looked bored as they ate, now used to the creole fare. Their mother was not in attendance, preferring her own company in her own quarters. After two years, she still refused to accept that this was now her life, her eyes always toward the harbor and the day she would sail with her children back to her homeland.

At sixteen, Felice no longer needed a tutor and Miss Rutherfurd quietly disappeared from the estate in what some would consider disgrace. For others, it was just another occurrence of life in the colony. Felice recalled the day the woman had fallen asleep in the middle of a lesson, the book she was poring over sliding to the floor. Finally, Felice could have her curiosity satisfied. *An Apology for the Conduct of Mrs. T. C. Phillips.*

Her own book forgotten, Felice delved in. Miss Rutherfurd stirred after a while. Quickly Felice stowed the book in the pocket of her dress and returned to her position at the small desk and back to reading *The History of Jamaica* by Edward

Long. Miss Rutherfurd searched high and low but did not dare ask Felice had she seen her book. After all, she should have been reading the book of religious poems within whose covers and pages the scandalous book had been disguised. She looked suspiciously at Felice whose young face proclaimed her innocence.

That night, Felice's eyes opened to a world far away and the scandalous life of a woman who had married her way through infamy. To think she had also lived on the island and made *Mistress of the Revels*. Five husbands! Her life was open and in the pages of a book for all to see. No wonder Miss Rutherfurd was so engaged in her reading. To live so free and do what you wanted! Somewhere inside of her, Felice wished she too could live her life the way she wanted instead of being locked up on an estate where she did not belong in one place or the other.

Then, the rumors had become true. Miss Rutherfurd had been carrying on with a free man of color named John Taylor. His wife Martha took to her bed when the discovery was made, her six children attending to her needs and hoping she would recover soon. Then, Miss Rutherfurd disappeared and soon news came that she and John Taylor were living together in Spanish Town.

"If *you* should have such a fate," Mary Henderson uttered with much vehemence toward Felice when news came of Miss Rutherfurd, surprising the young girl as she sat in the drawing room engrossed in the book she had read over and over since she had stolen it from Miss Rutherfurd. Felice had not seen Mary Henderson since then, although they lived in the same house. She was glad for that.

The dinner guests finally rose amid their chatter and headed toward the drawing room. Mulatto John walked purposefully toward Felice and seated her in an armchair. He sat across from her in a straight-backed chair. The room had been arranged by the servants for conversation.

"Hello, Felice," he said, a small smile on his mouth, his eyes twinkling as if delighted to see her.

His voice. His voice had become more like a man's. A cultivated voice at that.

"Where have you been, may I ask?" Felice finally asked, trying to match his gaze but failing, her eyes looking away from their disturbance.

"My father sent me to England."

"England?" she exclaimed.

It was a faraway place, she knew; one she never hoped to ever go to. It was too far away from everything she had known all her life; too far away from her mother and sister.

"Yes, my dear. He thought I needed an English education. He plans on making me his heir."

"Heir? What of the laws?"

"There are ways around everything. It so happens, dear Felice, that my mother is actually a mulatto, although a rather dark-skinned one with Negro hair. Thus, my dear, I am white by law."

He finished with a smile on his face and a note of pride in his voice. Felice's face fell. In that moment he felt so far removed from her reach. He was white by law and so could inherit vast amounts of property, even slaves, if his father made him his heir. He could have anyone he wanted for his wife. He could even return to England and find himself a wife. Maybe even now there was someone waiting for him to return to England for them to marry.

She had thought so much about him and had finally given him up for lost when no news came of him or from him. There had been a drowning in the Great River during the rainy season. She had hedged closer to Cook, her mother, to see if the woman would let anything drop about the mulatto son of Mr. McDowell. But Cook had only fussed at her until she decided it was no longer safe to be in the same room with the woman. It felt like now the secret was known, she did not want her next to her any longer. Was she ashamed of her?

The moment Mulatto John had arrived with his father for dinner that evening Felice had felt glad he had returned to her, even more handsome than before. Her breath had stopped and her heart beat faster as she watched him in his waistcoat and long sleeved shirt and woolen trousers, his hair with a neat part on one side, his whiskers and moustache trimmed. She hardly knew it was him in that moment.

"Have you missed me?" he asked as she sat silent.

"Yes," she whispered, a fluttering in her chest making her breathless.

"We should go riding again. Would you like that?"

"Yes."

"Tonight?"

"Yes."

"You have become a beautiful woman," he commented, watching the color rise on her face and her eyes flutter to look down at her hands folded in her lap.

And you have become bold, she thought. There was a small silence while the conversation flowed around them. Young Duncan and Rebecca had already been taken to bed by Aquila and the men were sitting in a circle across the room discussing business. Smoke wafted through the air and an occasional cough punctuated the conversation.

Felice looked up to meet her father's gaze through the haze of smoke. She could not read his clouded eyes but they were narrowed and looked like an idea might be forming behind them. She just hoped he was not planning on sending her to England. That would not do. That just would not do. She would rather run away

"So, what have you been doing with yourself?" John asked.

"I found my mother," she responded.

"You did?" he asked, an eyebrow raised. "Who, may I ask?"

"Cook?" she responded.

"The cook? How?"

"After you and I talked, I decided I must find out. She admitted to being my mother."

"How do you feel about that?"

"I have got used to it now. In the beginning, I was angry that she had not told me all these years. Now, it does not matter. I cannot change that she is my mother."

"So, that solves that. I was surprised to discover that my mother is a mulatto. I never gave it a second thought before. Now, I am able to inherit from my father."

"You are fortunate. What can I hope for my future? Become mistress of a rich white planter? It just is not fair."

"You can marry a rich mulatto."

"I certainly can't marry a Negro."

The group across the room rose noisily and the men began heading to the door. Mulatto John rose and inclined his head toward her.

Later that night, Felice slipped out the front door into the darkness. Mulatto John emerged from the shadows, his horse's reins in his hand. Silently, he helped her up onto the back of the beast, one arm gently pulling her against him, the other holding the reins as he guided the horse down to the river.

Their ride was a silent one, shadows of trees cloaking their progress. Felice could feel the heat of his body next to hers, his breath against her neck. It seemed they moved as one with the beast. She did not know how long or how far they rode but it seemed over too soon when they returned to the tamarind tree and he let her down. Her hand lingered for a moment in his and then she was running toward the house, conscious that he watched her retreat.

Felice awoke the following morning to the sound of rain and muffled voices from the drawing room. Quickly, she dressed and hurried down the stairs to find a group of men had gathered in discussion with her father in the drawing room. She stood just outside the door, pressing herself flat against the wall as she listened in on the discussion. It was clear the men were agitated.

"The ringleaders will be executed," a male voice declared emphatically.

"It's a good you found your boy loading the pistol, Chambers. Only God knows what would have happened to us all," McDowell congratulated.

"We would all be dead in our beds if you ask me," someone opined, his voice thick with his anger.

"Ungrateful wretches," ground another voice. "After all we do for them you would think they would only want to protect us."

"My own driver and domestics," moaned another in disbelief.

"We have been complacent for too long," Felice heard her father say. "Granted, mine have been a rather docile lot but I have a feeling there are some who participated in one way or another. I have my suspicions."

"We have entirely been too careless airing our grievances in front of them. They aren't all imbeciles, you know," McDowell growled.

"Right, McDowell. They knew the Regiment had left. We're outnumbered twenty-five to one here. God, man. Hang them one and all, if you ask me," someone bellowed.

"Used to be the new Negroes we had to worry about. Now the creoles have joined them. Heaven help us," McDowell declared.

Felice did not recognize the other voices but it was clear that rumors of a plot by the slaves to revolt had been foiled. It was the first time they had had such an uprising in this end of the island and worse it involved drivers and domestics among others and not just the field slaves or newly arrived slaves. It had been carefully planned, it seemed.

"What you doing here, Miss Felice?"

Felice jumped visibly at the harsh whisper. Cook stood before her, drenched from the rain and carrying a tray of Beveridge pitchers for the roomful of men. Next to her was Morgiana holding another tray with glasses. Morgiana gave her a shy smile.

Morgiana, a year younger, was as dark as Felice was brown with a head of thick hair, which she plaited in two and tucked behind her ears. Her face had, like Felice's, lost its baby fat and had narrowed to emphasize high cheekbones and softly curving lips. Her eyes were slanted and dark brown to mysterious black.

"Nothing. I heard the voices from up the stairs."

"Well, don't mek it a habit to listen in on odda people business. You might no like what you hear. Come, Morgie."

Morgiana nodded at Felice and followed Cook into the room. Felice stood for a moment as the room quieted at their entrance and she could hear the clink of glasses.

"Where *did* you find this one, Henderson?" one of the male voices commented with a chuckle. "Looks like a good breeder. Titties still firm. Good *cum*, you think?"

Loud guffaws followed. Cook hurried out of the room, her fury on her face. Huffing past Felice, Morgiana in her wake, she hurried out to her domain.

Felice retreated to her room, an anger boiling up inside her.

She could not believe that her father would allow them to speak of Morgie that way. Granted, he was not Morgie's father but his child was her sister; her mother his lover. What was Morgiana, anyway? She was just another slave as far as they cared.

In the following days, Felice heard some of the names of the perpetrators of the rebellion: Blue Hole Harry, Quamono, Peter, Charles, Prince, and Leander, all from other plantations. The plan had been to attack and take over the town of Lucea. No more hiding in the bushes for surprise attacks. They would become masters of their own destinies. Cudjoe's people would join them, they claimed. Only, that did not happen and utter confusion reigned. In the end, executions followed and some were transported. The rebellion put the plantation owners on notice that it was no longer the usual business.

Amid all this, there were disturbances on the Henderson plantation. There were rumors of Quaco, a Coramantee and his wife Mary and son Samson being a part of the rebellion. Young Samson was the age of Felice with his Coramantee blood boiling in his veins. Some said Quaco and Mary had been part of the rebellion in 1760. Mary herself had shot and killed a soldier. But those had only been rumors.

Mary had been forced from working the fields to working as a housemaid in the Great House because of an injury that had not been properly treated. Some said the injury had been caused by a gunshot she received one night as she sneaked from one plantation to the next, spreading word of a planned revolt.

The rustling in the bushes had startled the drunk, jittery Overseer, they said, and he had fired off shots. Quaco pleaded to be allowed to be by her side and he now worked also in the Great House as one of the housemen.

What would have happened to Felice herself, living in the Great House had the rebels succeeded in their plans? Only Cook could have saved her, she thought.

"Miss Felice," a voice called in a whisper from somewhere underneath the verandah.

Felice sat up, setting aside the book she had been reading. The estate was quiet since it was after crop time but there was a certain uneasiness after the quelled rebellion that left everyone on edge. The downfall of the rebels was their differences: the Ibos, the Coramantees, the creoles. And the Maroons. They all wanted different outcomes in their desire to reclaim themselves as a people. But that was just it; they were many different people. The kings and princes and the warriors could not agree across the divide; even their choice of weapon was different. And the whites, taking advantage, further divided and conquered them.

Visits between estates by whites were only for meetings to discuss plans on how to protect themselves and how to prevent the movement of the slaves between plantations. The planters were taking no chances with their lives and property, still reeling from their close encounter.

"Miss Felice," the voice called again.

"Morgie?"

"Yes, Miss Felice."

"What you doing here? You suppose to be working."

"They looking fi me."

"Whatever for?"

"They say I involve."

Morgiana had not yet shown her face and Felice did not like talking to a voice.

"Come on out, Morgie."

"No, Miss Felice. They will catch me."

"I will protect you, Morgie."

"Hmph. Nobody can protect me, Miss Felice. Least of all, you."

"I will speak with my father."

Felice became aware of a shadow behind her.

"Who are you speaking with?" a female voice demanded with a tone of suspicion to it.

Mary Henderson stood behind her. Felice had not seen her for some time and almost did not recognize the figure standing there.

Mary Henderson had grown rolls of fat on her body and her

face was as plump as the pig Cook threw scraps to outside the cookhouse.

"No one, Missis," Felice assured as she stood and curtsied.

"I heard voices."

"It was just some chickens loose from the fowl house, Missis. I was shooing them back."

"I don't believe you. Are you harboring a man?"

"No, Missis."

"That's all you are good for anyway. Breed like the animals. Don't think I am finished with you."

With that the woman rolled away and back into the house. What had made her decide to emerge from her quarters to stroll the estate this morning?

Felice waited until she was sure the woman had left before calling out to Morgiana. But there was silence and she hoped her sister had escaped to safety.

What would make Morgie want to join the rebels? She lived in the Great House, for God's sake, Felice thought. Her mother was the cook and she never wanted for food. Felice recalled times when Cook would bring a treat out from its hiding place; maybe cut coconut and sugar she had dropped on banana leaf that day. Or a length of sweet sugar cane they would sometimes sit on the back steps at night to chew on while everyone else was abed. They would watch the night sky and wonder how far it went and what it would be like to float high up above like the birds did. Maybe someday they could fly away to a place of freedom for them all. Maybe.

Although Morgie had worked the fields as soon as she was old enough, when she got home, her life was a little different from all the other slaves. She had a good bed made of *coir* to sleep on. Not like the banana trash some had to make do with in their huts. Duncan Henderson took care of his slaves. Why would anyone want to kill him?

The following morning a gathering under the tamarind tree greeted Felice as she came down the stairs and walked outside. Her heart gave a small leap as she recognized Morgiana in the crowd, her hands tied behind her back, her clothes dirty and tattered like she had been dragged through the bushes and the dirt. Felice ran toward her and the small crowd parted to reveal three other prisoners similarly bound.

"What is going on?" she asked in a voice she had perfected from her years of training with Miss Rutherfurd.

"You stay out of this, Miss Felice," the muscular black man Felix commanded, a whip in hand.

"How dare you? She is my sister. I will not have her treated this way."

"Miss Felice, dis is none of your business," the man responded as he stood menacingly, guarding his charges.

"I demand you set her free at once!"

"Dat is not for you to decide, Miss Felice."

"What is going on here?" Duncan Henderson boomed, appearing larger than life before the crowd. "Felice?"

The crowd began drifting away; after all, there was work to be done on the estate. They did not have the luxury of time off because some had decided to join the rebels and fight for their freedom.

"Why are they holding Morgiana this way?" she demanded of her father, her commanding voice sounding strange to her own ears.

"Get back to the house, Felice," Henderson ordered.

Felice hesitated and then marched away toward the cookhouse. Cook was coming across the yard toward her. The woman did not seem to see Felice as she advanced toward the crowd to stand next to Duncan Henderson. Arms at her kimbo, Cook stood, legs planted firmly and in silence. Felice stood watching the scene. In that moment, her mother seemed not unlike one of the warriors she often heard talked about: the Maroons.

"Release *her*," Duncan Henderson finally commanded as he nodded toward Morgiana. "Forty each, Felix. And that's that."

Abruptly, he left, returning to the Great House. Looking up, he saw Mary Henderson in the shadow of her verandah, watching. Ignoring her, he continued to his study where the bookkeeper was waiting. There was business of the estate to be conducted. Mary Henderson was the least of his concerns just now. The books were not looking too good right now. He could not afford to fail.

Grabbing Morgiana's arm, Cook began dragging her away but the girl stood firm, refusing to be moved. Quaco, Mary, and Samson were tied separately to branches on the tamarind tree, their backs exposed. They stood resolute and straight-backed. Samson's eyes met Morgiana's, their expression unclear. Then he turned away, his chin held high as he braced himself, his eyes up to heaven.

Two muscled men appeared from behind the crowd, whips in hand. The first blow came to Quaco's back, already welted and healed; welted and healed again. The rhythm of leather on flesh was all that could be heard as each was whipped in turn. Samson refused to look at his mother as she finally slumped senseless. He knew his father's muscles bulged rigidly, his shiny dark skin deflecting the blows with the power of his mind. That was how Quaco had taught his son. From somewhere in his youth Quaco recalled the ways he had survived the crossing and before. And the afterward in a land that still did not belong to him; a land he could never hope to own even a small piece of.

Samson had long learned to not fear the whip. It was the fear that made the blows harder to bear, Quaco told his son. He no longer heard the voices of the men counting, or the gasps of the young children who were, for the first time witnessing the punishment that no doubt would be meted out to them many times during their lifetime for such offences as looking at their master the wrong way.

Felice gasped audibly. She had heard of it but had never seen it. She could not believe her father had ordered this; and to be done to poor Mary who could barely walk anyway. How could this be? She thought of Morgiana and how she also would have been whipped had their mother not stepped in. How could this be? She had only known her father to be a kind man. He treated everyone fairly, she thought. How could Duncan Henderson do such a thing to other human beings?

Blood was oozing down the backs of the three but they did not utter a cry, only deep, soft grunts meant to comfort. Felice moved to stand behind Cook so she would not have to see anymore. She felt the tears trickling from her eyes as she prayed for the sounds to stop. Finally, there was silence and Morgiana ran forward, falling to her knees next to Samson. Felice peeked from behind her mother.

Quaco, Mary, and Samson were slumped against the tree and panic swept through Felice. Had they killed them?

"Samson," Morgiana called in a loud whisper to the silent figure.

There was no response. Someone hurried forward with a pail of water and a rag and handed it to Morgiana. The girl wet the rag and squeezed out the excess water before gently wiping Samson's face. He stirred. Pulling a sharp knife from her waist, Morgiana swiftly sliced through the ropes that held him bound and he slid to his knees. Cupping her hands, Morgiana scooped water from the pail and brought it to his lips. The liquid dripped between her fingers as he quickly wet his lips and closed his eyes for a moment.

Two women attended to Quaco and Mary, wiping them down. Then a man known as Dallas scooped Mary up to take her away to her hut. Bravely, Quaco rose to his feet and staggered painfully behind.

"Morgie," Cook called to her daughter.

Morgiana looked up but did not move.

"Come, girl," Cook insisted.

Morgiana did not move but continued ministering to Samson. Cook hissed her teeth and walked away. Felice stood, unsure if she should follow Cook or remain with her sister.

Morgiana's already torn and dusty dress was covered with blood. Her hands cradled Samson's head and she was singing softly to him. Felice could not make out the words she was singing but it sounded like another tongue. Suddenly, Samson heaved himself upright and, with the raised weals on his back now thick with drying blood, stood like a man for his sixteen years. With Morgiana by his side, Samson limped away.

The Master's Daughter   Vjange Hazle

CHAPTER 5

Felice lay on her canopied bed that night unable to sleep, the scenes of the day playing in her head again and again. Outside a riot of crickets and toads called from the bushes. The estate seemed so quiet now; but the turmoil inside Felice's head would not let up.

Was it her good fortune to have been born a mulatto? Did mulattos ever get whipped? She still could not believe what she had witnessed. She had heard talk of whippings but had never been witness to one. Her stomach still churned and it was as if she could still hear the sound of the whip cutting into flesh. She could still see the blood and hear the soft moans. Being a woman had not spared Mary. Poor woman.

Morgiana had disappeared with Samson and was not in the room she still shared with Cook the last Felice checked before coming up the stairs and to her own bed. Did Morgie care for Samson? Had she gone to take care of him? What of Quaco and Mary? Who was attending to them?

How could someone beat another human senseless? Yes, they were slaves; but were they not also human? She thought of Morgiana and felt a slight anger toward her sister. Why did she have to go and join the rebels? Why could she not be content with her life? She had food and a roof over her head, for God's sake.

Her anger toward Morgiana was quickly replaced by another: anger at the white people who made slaves of people like her mother and sister. She recalled those days as children when she and Morgie would romp together, unaware that they were sisters sharing the same mother. Felice had not even been aware then that there was a difference in the color of their skin.

Did Mulatto John know that things like this happened? She wanted so to talk with him but, with the events occurring across the island, it was not safe for anyone to travel about. There was still rampant fear of another rebellion, although some of the ringleaders had been caught and there was talk of whippings, transportation, and executions. Many were turning on each other and they were using the Maroons to hunt out other leaders for court trial.

Felice had seen Mr. McDowell as he and her father met; but Mulatto John would never accompany him to these meetings. Like her, he did not belong to any side. They were neither Negro nor white. No one wanted them. But, they also had to be protected by those who had sired them.

Felice hoped she would see Mulatto John soon. Their night rides had been too few. When he pulled her close to his body, she felt like she belonged. Her body went warm, hot, and all she wanted to do was fold herself into him.

His revelation to her at their last meeting put a small fear inside her. Now that he discovered he was white by law, maybe he would not want to be around her anymore.

Maybe he would find himself a white wife to bear his children; and with his inheritance he could become a wealthy man much sought after. He did not even have to remain on the island if he did not want to. What if he had returned to England without her knowledge?

Felice tossed in her bed feeling the cool night air coming through the open window, slightly stirring the nets. She knew the mosquitoes were dancing somewhere but she was safe behind her net. It had not always been that way. Felice thought of her sister and wondered if where she slept she was safe from the mosquitoes. It wasn't fair. It just wasn't fair.

The morning sun rose bright like it always did most days in the tropical island. Before sunrise, the slaves had already attended to their piece of ground before going off to the cane fields, which now lay fallow. It was how they had fed themselves during the mean years and how the planters had kept their profits in their pockets. With the price of beef and flour almost doubling, they had to find a way to keep their way of living and their slaves occupied. Slaves were expensive to feed they were discovering. The best solution was to give them their own piece of ground, not too much for them to get rich themselves, just enough to plant the food they and their families cooked and ate.

Dressing quickly, Felice headed down the stairs toward the cookhouse. Cook stirred a pot of porridge in the black, sooted pot, her face a surly darkness as she hummed a dark tune. She glanced at Felice and turned back to her task.

"Where is Morgie?" Felice demanded.

"Why you asking me?" Cook responded without looking at her.

"How you mean why?" Felice demanded.

"Felice, doan bodda mi soul dis morning."

"You don't care where your daughter has gone to?"

"Felice. Leave Morgiana business alone."

"I can't believe you just let her go like that."

"Listen to me, Felice. You cannot undastan what going on. It better you go back to di house an to you room an leave it alone. Missa Henderson provide fi you. Tek it an ask no question."

"I can't believe you. I am going to search for Morgie myself."

"Felice!"

Cook's voice was a heavy command and Felice stopped in her tracks.

"What?"

"I warning you, leave it alone. Dis is bigga dan you, Felice. Leave it alone, I say."

Felice wheeled from the cookhouse. She must find her sister. She must know what happened to her. Hurrying through the front door of the Great House, she headed toward the field.

The sun had not yet fully risen as she passed the workers

already bent low in the field. Blackened scrubs dotted the expanse along with the bent figures distinguishable only because of their clothes. Heads rose to note her progress and then bent to their task again before the overseer noticed.

The path she trod was familiar. As children, she and Morgie had run around with the other children their age. They had often gone to the slave huts to play in the open dirt space over which women, old, toothless, crippled, and no longer able to work the fields often presided. The children were free to roam and often wandered off as soon as the women dozed off. They would hear their cackling voices time and again calling them back to safety. Maybe an old woman would know where Morgie was.

Felice could hear the squeals of children at their noisy play as she approached the thatched huts. Some were still asleep, wrapped in sheets and plumped up in baskets. An old woman sat in the dirt, a clay pipe lodged in a corner of her mouth. The scent of tobacco greeted Felice.

"Good morning," Felice greeted in her best voice as she approached the woman.

Sightless eyes looked up at her.

"Who dat?" the woman called.

"I am looking for Morgie, ma'am. Morgiana. Cook's daughter."

"Who looking fa har?"

"Me, ma'am. Felice. The Master's daughter."

"Why you want har?"

"She's my sister."

The woman was silent.

"Why you want har?" the woman insisted as she puffed on her pipe.

"I am concerned if she is alright."

"You modda know you here?"

"Yes, ma'am," Felice lied. "She sent me to see about Morgie."

"I doan believe you, yuh know. But I gwine tell you. You know where Mary live?"

"No, ma'am."

"Go roun di corner til you ketch to a mango tree. Is right dere so."

"Tanks, ma'am."

The woman's darkened eyes seemed to follow her progress as Felice walked away. The settlement was quiet except for the sounds of the children's play. Felice wasn't sure which hut belonged to Mary but, as she approached, Morgiana emerged from one, a pail in hand. The girl stopped in her tracks.

"Morgie," Felice called as she started toward her.

Morgiana's stare stopped Felice's forward movement.

"Miss Felice. What you doing here?"

"Morgie, I came to see you are alright. How are you feeling?"

"I am alright."

"How are they?"

"How you think?"

"I am so sorry, Morgie."

"Sorry?"

"My father…"

"Yes, *your* father."

Felice hung her head. Then she raised it again and stared her sister in the eyes. Who was Morgiana's father anyway?

"Listen, Morgiana. I have no control over what my father does. You are my sister and I care to see that you are alright. What can I do to help?"

"Well, you can fetch water."

"F-fetch water?"

"Yes. You can do dat?"

Felice stared at her sister.

"Morgie, you know full well that I have never fetched water in my whole life," Felice finally said with a chuckle.

A broad smile came across Morgiana's face and both sisters embraced.

"Dem in so much pain," Morgiana said with a small groan.

"What can I do?" Felice asked again.

"Go inside until I come back."

Obediently, Felice entered the darkness of the hut. She could smell the staleness of flesh and ointments she could not identify. A small window let in some sunlight. Felice looked around and her eyes began to become accustomed to the dimness. There was a small shuffle and Felice glanced at the floor from where the sound came. Samson lay on his stomach in the middle of the room, his head raised to see who had entered. Next to him lay Quaco on his side facing the entrance. His eyes were closed. Mary lay on the bed, her back, raw and red, turned to the door.

Felice stood, uncertain what to do. She wished Morgie would hurry back. She heard a slight sound and glanced around to where a figure sat in a corner, her knees drawn up to her chest. A moment of fear seized Felice as the eyes bored into hers.

The woman seemed larger than life where she sat. The whites of her large eyes seemed to glow in the half-darkness.

Her dark face and broad forehead were framed by a mass of wooly hair that was wrapped with a slender white band. Her cheekbones were pronounced and her slightly protruding lips had a firm set. It was impossible to tell how old she was but Felice thought she and Cook might be the same age.

"Good morning," Felice ventured.

The woman gave a slight nod of her head and turned away as if in disgust, her eyes fixed on a spot on the opposite wall. The silence in the room was making Felice uncomfortable. A shadow darkened the doorway and Morgiana entered and helped herself down with the pail of water, placing it on the dirt floor before removing the *kotta* made of banana trash from her head.

The girl bustled around the room in silence, grabbing two basin pans from their hiding place under the bed. The woman rose and Felice's eyes widened. She had never seen a woman so tall and strapping. She was like a warrior woman. Who was she?

Pouring water into one of the pans, the woman walked over to Mary and squatted. After mopping Mary's welted back, she dried it with an old dress and began rubbing a liquid across the woman's back. Mary made soft whimpering sounds, her body shivering.

"How can I help?" Felice asked in a whisper.

"I think you better go back to di house, Miss Felice," Morgiana replied softly as she stooped to where Samson lay on the floor, her eyes staring at the back of the woman's head.

Felice hesitated. Morgiana stared at her pointedly. Not understanding, Felice turned to the door, her eyes on the stiffness of the woman's back. She walked out into the bright sunshine, her eyes watering for a moment. Felice blinked and the water dried up.

This was not the Morgie she knew. They had romped together as children, not knowing that they were sisters from the same mother. Only a year younger, Morgie had early on attached herself to Felice and the two had become steadfast friends and companions; where there was one there was the other. They slept in the same bed; or more often in Cook's bed, especially when the night rain and winds howled outside. They had run together through the dirt and dust of the yard with Felice always calling "Come, Morgie" and grabbing the little girl's hand. Before Morgie was sent to the fields to work, they had raided the fruit trees together and had often returned to Cook to be cleaned up, fed, and put to bed. Now, Felice wasn't sure she knew this almost woman Morgie had become.

As Felice walked back to the Great House, she wondered if Cook knew what her daughter was doing. And, who was that woman who sent shivers down her spine?

Felice hurried toward the stairs of the Great House, determined to change into fresh clothes. Mary Henderson emerged from the drawing room, Aquila lingering behind her.

Felice curtsied and attempted to pass but the woman stood firmly in front of her. Aquila stood poised in a dress her mistress had been able to fit into maybe two years before; her feet were bare.

"Where have you been?" Mary Henderson inquired, looking down at Felice.

"I went for a walk, Missis," Felice replied, looking down at the floor.

"Are you meeting a man?"

"No, Missis."

"Hmmm. You better not bring any pickneys in here, understand. That will not be tolerated under my roof."

"Yes, Missis."

Felice sensed a change in the atmosphere but was not sure who had come up behind her.

"What are *you* doing here?" Mary Henderson demanded of the new arrival.

"I come to get Felice, Missis," Cook responded almost too quietly.

"Whatever for?"

Cook stood silent, staring her missis in the eye.

A movement caught Felice's eye and she realized that her father had emerged from the study.

"Whatever is going on here?" Duncan Henderson asked in a low voice as he stared from one woman to the other, his hands folded behind his back.

"Your cook does not know her place, Duncan," Mary Henderson explained haughtily.

"And what is that, pray tell, my dear wife?"

"She walks in here as if she owns the place for God's sake."

"She is the cook, remember."

"But that does not give her access to my house any time she wants. She belongs in the cook house among the black pots and pans and should enter *only* when she is summoned."

Felice could feel the heat coming from Cook.

"Isabella, was there something you needed?" Henderson inquired, turning to Cook.

"Felice."

"Well, go ahead."

"Come, Miss Felice," Cook ordered.

Felice hesitated as she watched the flare of Mary Henderson's nostrils. She felt she could see the steam blowing from them.

The woman's chest heaved and Felice worried that she would surely fall to the floor in a heap. Behind her, Aquila stood with her mouth open as if she had a comment she needed to make but thought better of it. Grabbing her hand, Cook pulled at Felice and the girl followed obediently.

Cook did not stop until they both were in the cookhouse where the woman seated Felice on a small bench.

"Felice. I want you to listen to me and listen to me good. You mus nevah bow to dat woman," Cook commanded, wagging a finger in Felice's face. "She might be white but she no betta dan you. De same blood run through yuh vein. Doan mek she run you outa di house, yuh hear me?"

"But..."

"Doan but me, chile. I say, you not to let dat debbil woman mek you get put outa road. Undastan? Missa Henderson is yuh fadda. Yuh here long before she. Is time yuh stan up to har."

"But how? She is missis."

"So she tink. So she tink. Where you been all morning?"

Felice was silent. Cook was confusing her.

"I ask you a question."

"I don't have to tell you anything."

"Felice!"

"Alright! I went to see Morgie."

"Didn't I tell yuh is none of yuh business? Felice, leave it alone."

"But they need help."

"Dey can help demself. Felice, dese are tings dat is none of your business. You is not a slave. You is a free woman dat can married any odda malatta pon di island."

Free? She was free? Free while her sister and mother were slaves? How could that be? She was free to marry any mulatto on the island. Did that include Mulatto John?

"What are you saying, Cook?"

"Felice, your fadda sign di papers. I make sure. I might not can read but I ask Morgie to look pon it an it say you free."

"When did this happen? How come I was not told?" Felice demanded.

"When Missa Henderson decide you should have yuh own room in di house him draw up di papers."

"But, what about you and Morgie?"

"Worry about yuhself, Felice."

"Why should you and Morgie still be enslaved?"

"Someday, Felice. Someday."

Isabella's eyes took on a faraway look as if she saw that she too would someday walk the road of the free in this land her mother's parents had been brought to in chains; as if she and Morgie would walk side by side with the child she had given birth to in the year of Tacky's rebellion as equals sometime in the future. Tacky himself had died in that rebellion as had so many others since then. Freedom had not yet come.

"I am going to ask my father to free you and Morgie."

"But what a hard head chile yuh is, eeh Felice. Massa will nevah free me."

"Why?"

"Aaah, dere is some tings you will nevah undastan, Miss Felice. All I want to tell you is to be careful of dat woman. Doan figet yuh is as free as she is."

"I am still going to speak with my father."

"Felice, tell me something. If Missa Henderson write up paper fi free me an Morgie, where we going to go? What we going to do? We have food, clothes, and bed fi sleep in. We have a roof ova wi head. Massa been good to me. I doan want fi nuttin. Morgie doan want fi nuttin. I doan undastan why she join wid dem people an want fi fight."

Felice sat silent. She thought of Morgie standing vigil over Samson and his parents. Why had Morgie decided to fight? Cook was right; she had all she ever wanted. She was being ungrateful.

But did she have the freedom to live her life the way Felice did? Would she ever be anything other than a slave?

CHAPTER 6

"Martial Law!" bellowed McDowell. "It's about bloody time."

"We are about to be murdered here, man," a red-faced planter called Jenkins added, a note of a tremor in his voice.

"Chambers, you are a lucky man, indeed," Henderson commented. "Had you not foiled the man, every white person would have lay dead in their beds. Providence, man. Providence."

Felice listened to the conversation around the table, her eyes fixed on the empty space where Mulatto John would most certainly have been sitting. Rebecca and Young Duncan sat in their usual places. She was amazed at how they had grown in the past two years; Rebecca was outgrowing her dresses and Duncan's trousers were now a bit short for his legs.

Mary Henderson sat at the other end of the table from her husband. Her light cotton gowns were now being made by her personal seamstress using fabric she had sent for from England. Her eyes remained on Felice throughout the evening.

Felice wanted to ask after Mulatto John but it would be unseemly to do so. No mention was made of him throughout the dinner and she groaned inwardly. Was he now betrothed to some white woman or a pretty mulatto? Had he been sent away again to England?

The food had no taste in her mouth and it seemed a long time before the men rose to go to the drawing room. Felice excused herself to her room and rushed up the stairs away from the fiery darting swords of Mary Henderson's glares. She sank onto her bed and stared up at the canopy as if for answers.

Where was Mulatto John? Had he been hurt in the rebellion? The insurrections were all over the island and the slaves did not seem ready to give in. They were burning down plantations all across the island and creating havoc for the planters.

The fact that no mention was made of Mulatto John must mean that he was alright, Felice concluded. His father would most certainly have spoken of his son having come to harm.

Restless, she rose and went to the open window to gaze at the sultry night. The darkness greeted her and she wondered where Morgiana was. She had not seen her sister this past week and she had not heard word of how her charges were doing. Cook had refused to discuss the matter any further. The mosquitoes buzzed at her ears and Felice swatted at them.

How she longed to hear the sound of his horse's snorts and feel the animal beneath her. Where was Mulatto John? Felice sighed as she changed into her nightclothes. She wondered what Mary Henderson would do if she found out about her nighttime rides with John. She would most certainly fall in a fit and die. A small smile came to her lips.

The Master's Daughter   Vjange Hazle

Heavy rains pounded the estate that night and Felice prayed it was not a hurricane. How she wished she could curl up next to Cook on a night such as this. The lightning and thunder flashed and rolled in their fury, lighting up the night and clapping like some giant roaming over the land. Covering her head with her pillow, Felice tried to shut it all out. Her thoughts came again to Morgiana.

Her sister and mother were not free. It just was not fair. She herself could not free them. Perhaps someday she could buy them to be her own slaves; but it just did not seem right to enslave your own mother and sister. Maybe if she spoke to her father. But Cook had forbidden her to. And she was right: what would she and Morgie do as free people? They had no money; no land. They were, perhaps, better off enslaved.

Felice turned in her bed, her nightgown sticking to her body. The rain had not made the night any cooler. She was still afraid of her father and wondered how Cook could stand up to him so, especially knowing he was her master and could whip her or sell her to anyone he wanted, even transport her to America of some other place. Just thinking about approaching him made her sweat and her breath come shallow.

But she remembered the one moment when she had seen her sister tied up like an animal, like one hunted out of the bushes, and how she had rushed to Morgie's defense. She had demanded answers from him then even though it was Cook who had saved Morgie from a whipping.

Why did he bow to the woman so when he made his own wife, his equal, cower in fear? What power did Cook have over Duncan Henderson?

Felice finally fell into a restless slumber and awoke to the sun's rays coming through her window. Hurrying down the stairs so that she would not be late for breakfast, she bumped into Morgiana carrying in the breakfast trays.

"Morgie!" she called softly.

"Good morning, Miss Felice. You ready to eat?"

"Yes, thank you."

Felice's eyes searched Morgie's but the girl continued with her duties as if they were simply mistress and servant. Felice followed her into the dining room.

"Is everything alright?" Felice continued.

"Yes, Miss Felice. Cook say must eat yuh breakfast."

Duncan Henderson sat waiting at the table.

"Good morning, Missa Henderson," Morgiana greeted almost cheerfully and with a small curtsy.

"Good morning, Morgiana. What has Isabella prepared for breakfast this morning?"

"Cassava bread di way yuh like it, sah."

She lifted the cover of the plate and the aroma of cooked liver rose in the room. The children arrived for breakfast but their mother was nowhere to be found. Felice was glad to not have to feel the weight of the woman's hateful stare in this early morning. The children seemed to have got used to her and were almost friendly toward her. Rebecca even threw her a smile across the table. Morgiana placed the food on the table and Nancy arrived with the beverages. Behind her Cook came bustling in.

"Everyting alright, Missa Henderson?" she asked, glancing at Felice.

"Yes, fine, thank you, Isabella. We are all satisfied here," he responded as he picked up his knife and fork. "Children, eat up."

The children dutifully did as they were told and breakfast felt almost like a pleasant affair. But Felice could not wait for it to be over. She wanted to talk with Morgie. How was she now serving in the house and not working out in the fields? What about her charges Quaco, Mary, and Samson? And who was that woman who made Felice feel like she could be pounced upon at any moment?

Felice hurried to the cookhouse as soon as she finished eating. She must speak with Morgiana. But her sister was busy helping Cook clean up and Nancy was scraping the scraps off the plates into a basin.

"What you want now, Miss Felice?" Cook asked.

"Nothing. I just came to see that everything was alright."

"Everything alright, Miss Felice. Doan worry yuhself," Morgiana assured.

Felice wheeled out of the room. It felt like there was a secret they shared between them that she was not a part of. A restlessness was overtaking her. Everyone else seemed to have something to do. Even the children were occupied with their new tutor, a tall, thin mulatto man named Brooks who had been educated in England and was now back on the island, hoping that his father would consider him as an heir since he was his only son. He had taken one look at Felice and dismissed her presence with his nose high in the air as if she was not of his ilk.

Taking a book from a pile in her room, Felice found a seat on the verandah outside of the drawing room and sat down to read. She could hear voices singing in the distance. There was something about the faraway sound that comforted her. She could not make out the words but she knew one man sang a line and everyone else sang after him. It was not a song of happiness, but the rhythm helped to make the work lighter. There was a time she had known some of those songs and she and Morgie had made them part of their everyday play. Now, it seemed she had forgotten them.

"Miss Felice," a voice called in a loud whisper.

"Morgie?"

Morgiana approached the verandah and Felice rose to look down at where her sister stood in the grass. The front of the girl's dress was dirty from cleaning.

"What happened, Morgie?"

"Cook convince Missa Henderson dat it betta to keep me near di house."

"You no longer work in the fields?"

"No," Morgie responded, a note of triumph in her voice.

"Good. How are Quaco and Mary and Samson?"

"Dem doing betta."

"Morgie, you musn't fight anymore, you hear?"

Morgiana stared at her sister.

"You can talk, Miss Felice."

"Morgie, please. You could be killed."

"Betta dan being a slave."

"Morgie, no. You cannot say that. It's not that bad for you."

"Miss Felice, you doan undastan dis ting. You will neva undastan dis ting. You live in a big house wid everyting you want. You is Massa dawta. Mos' of all, you free. Free fi walk as you want. Nobody fi beat you."

"Morgie, stop. I don't want to see you hurt."

"Miss Felice, some of us must get hurt. Some of us *gwine* get hurt. Dere is nutting dat say dat anybody have di right fi mek somebody else a slave. Nutting!" Morgiana said with much vehemence.

Felice glanced around, hoping nobody else could hear them.

"Morgie, please…"

"Me have to get back to work…"

"Morgie, wait!"

Morgiana paused.

"The woman in the hut the other day. Who is she?"

"You mean Mino? She a Popo woman."

"Popo?"

"She come from Popo country. She use to fight fi di Popo king but he punish har by selling har. She not too long come."

"You not afraid of her?"

"At first but she only fight di white people dem. Doan worry. You no white."

Morgiana walked away with a laugh. Felice watched her sister leave, the laughter echoing in her ears. *I might not be white, but I am free,* Felice thought as she watched the girl walk away, her back straight as if her blackness made her proud.

The trials were over; the executions done with. Names and bodies hung like a black wall of shame across the island. Some planters, convinced their own slaves were planning their own rebellions, executed the suspects. There was not much they needed to go by; they had to set an example, after all. One mulatto man in the east reported that the Moore Town Maroons were planning an insurrection. His untruth was soon revealed but not before much alarm resulted in severe punishments on slaves for certain acts of rebellion.

The slaves had planned their rebellion for the moment the regiment left the island unguarded, news of the declaration of their independence by the American colonies ringing in their ears. Their leaders were slaves in high places, creoles who had known nothing but enslavement but who were tired and hungry for food and freedom. Revolution was in the air; success was within their reach like it was for the American colonies. But victory was denied them and one by one they faced the judgment of their enslavers who lamented their insolence and ingratitude. Burnt alive, gibbeted, or hanged, their bodies swayed in the Jamaica breeze like so many fruits to be gazed upon but not tasted.

By Christmas, the island was settling back to its usual. Felice found herself in the flurry of preparation on the estate. The dirt path was trampled and swept, the tree roots whitewashed and the scent of cooking and baking filled the air that was no longer tinged with the smell of the shed blood and rotting flesh of the executed, gone and forgotten.

Felice thought of her sister Morgiana and how she too might have been one of those executed along with Quaco, Mary and Samson. It would serve her right. Her sister's remarks still stung. *You no white*. She never claimed to be white but she could not claim to be like her sister either, though they were of the same mother. Caught somewhere in between, Felice felt she did not belong anywhere.

Well, she would show her. *Who* was going to the ball in a gown now being fashioned and made by Mrs. Roper, the best seamstress in the north of the island? Certainly not Morgiana. The thought did not give Felice much satisfaction but she was content with what little it gave her. A feeling of excitement was building up in her as she thought of the *soirée* planned for the eve of Christmas Day at Mr. McDowell's estate.

Would she see Mulatto John? It was hard not to call him Mulatto John, even though he was really not a mulatto. Who else was going to be there, she wondered. She had never been to a ball before. In fact, she had never been off the estate and it gave her a feeling of anticipation. Will he want to talk to her or will he snub her? So much could have happened since she saw him last. He might even introduce her to his new wife. The thought sat bitterly somewhere in her gut.

Felice awoke early the morning of the ball and hurried down the stairs for her breakfast. Morgie floated in and out of the dining room with a smile pasted to her face and a nod for Felice who ignored her. The children sat petulant; they wanted to go to the ball but were told they were too young. Instead, they were to be sat by Aquila, the black, black-skinned woman whom they hated. Only they knew between them why.

Mary Henderson was confined to her quarters, having awakened vomiting terribly. She was pale and nothing she partook of was staying down in her stomach. She worried she might have caught some deadly disease from one of the natives and worried she would never again see her beloved homeland. Doctor Bayly was called and he ordered her to rest. Perhaps she should forgo the ball. But her gown hung in the wardrobe, a voluminous outfit complete with lace and various frills that she had designed herself. She would be at the ball, even if it killed her.

Quaco's Mary was assigned to Felice for the balance of day. The woman's back had healed but she still walked with a limp. As she recalled the beating and the small whimpers that came from Mary's lips, Felice wondered if the woman would ever think to rebel again. The figure curled up on the small bed in the semidarkness of the hut was in pain, she knew, and it had taken Morgiana's and Mino's ministrations to make her well again. Why would anyone want to go through that again?

"Good morning, Miss Felice," Mary greeted after knocking on the girl's room door before entering. "I come to take care of you today."

"Are you alright, Mary?" Felice asked the woman standing uncertainly in front of her.

"Yes, ma'am."

"Tell me something, Mary. Were you really involved in the uprisings?"

The woman was silent and it seemed she wrestled with her answer.

"Miss Felice, I come to help you today. I need to wash you hair an prepare you bath."

"I asked you a question, Mary, and I demand a response."

"Miss Felice, there are some things somebody like you wi neva undastan."

"*Why does everyone tell me I don't understand?* Maybe if someone explained to me I would understand," Felice exploded.

"Miss Felice, when you a slave in dis place, das all you is. I know what freedom feel like. I wasn' always a slave, ma'am."

"You weren't born in the colony?"

"No ma'am. I am di daughta of a chief. I was suppose to marry di son of a chief. Den dey grab me an bring me here. I was wid child den. Quaco tek care a me an Samson from di ship all di way to here. Quaco is a good man. Him doan deserve to be a slave either."

Felice was silent. What if she herself had been born a slave like Morgie? Would she now be in rebellion or would she have just accepted her lot? It was an uneasy thought and Felice dismissed it. How was it possible to imagine yourself a slave when all you have ever known is freedom? And privilege.

Mary went about her work, bringing the pails of water in to pour into the large wooden bath and to wash Felice's curls. Then she brushed them until they could bounce back no more for a while. She piled Felice's hair high on her head but the curls kept escaping, causing it to fall back down. Finally, Mary decided on a simple hairstyle that left Felice's curls mostly free. She placed a large bow at the back of the girl's head and pinned it into place.

The woman worked in silence and Felice did not disturb her. Felice wanted to ask her about Mino but was afraid to break into the uneasiness of the quietness. Mary was gentle with her and spoke only to issue small commands like 'turn dis way' or 'ben you head'.

Mary powdered Felice's body before gently lifting the gown over her head. Covering the front of the gown with a towel, Mary began applying cosmetics to the girl's face. Felice gazed at herself in the looking glass, marveling at the woman now appearing before her eyes.

Her complexion had become more white and her cheeks colored with a circular rosy rouge. Her lips were reddened and her eyebrows darkened. Had she not known it was herself she would have thought a white woman was sitting across from her. Finally, Felice stood, the gown flowing around her.

Her gown was a simple silk floral with a scooped neckline and puffed sleeves and at the back was a large bow. Felice gazed at her image and how the skirt of her gown showed off her broadening hips. Reaching for a package on the bureau, Felice pulled the string and the wrapping fell away to reveal a box.

Duncan Henderson had handed the box to her as they finished breakfast that morning. Rebecca and young Duncan sat astonished as he had pushed the package toward her with a grunt. The children glanced at each other as if they were saving this bit of news to be passed on somewhere else.

Felice had not opened it then; but now as she lifted the cover of the box she saw a pearl brooch inside. She ran her finger over the piece of jewelry. She had never seen or touched pearls before. Removing the brooch from its place of safety, Felice handed it to Mary to be pinned on her bosom.

"You look nice, Miss Felice," Mary commented as she surveyed the young woman, her job complete. "You could almos' pass fi a white woman."

"Thank you, Mary."

A knock sounded on the door as Felice paraded in front of the mirror, trying to recognize herself as the same person. Mary opened the door and Samson stood in the hallway.

"I come to take you to di ball, Miss Felice," the young man said, his cap in his hand.

He was indeed handsome, Felice thought as he stood there, head bowed. He looked so different from the young man she had seen tied up and being beaten and then again laying on the floor of his parents' hut in pain. His wounds must have healed like Mary's had. Now she understood why Morgie had stood by him. Dressed in his livery, his stature that of a man almost fully formed, he did not look like a slave; one who needed to fight for his freedom. He looked like a prince who would someday rule his people with a firm hand and much dignity.

"She soon come down, Samson," Mary advised and he hurried away as his mother shut the door behind him.

The traveling coach stood in front of the door of the Great House, its horse stomping impatiently. Felice paused uncertainly at the top of the front steps, gazing down at the upturned faces of the gathered slaves who had come to watch her go. She recognized most of them; some were from her childhood. There were others who perhaps had come to the estate later on. They all seemed so dusty and dark. Absently, Felice wondered what they would look like if they had the chance to wash themselves and wear the finery only available to their masters, their feet shod.

At the head of the steps stood Cook and Morgiana side by side, Cook's face wreathed in smiles, her stance one reflecting a mother's pride. Felice smiled back at her mother and made to rush toward her for an embrace. The stern look that crossed Cook's face stopped her in her tracks. Nodding at both her mother and sister, Felice proceeded toward the coach where Samson stood waiting in his black breeches and yellow embroidered waistcoat.

Ahead of Felice's coach stood another into which Mary Henderson and her gown were being piled. Felice's carriage slowly pulled away behind the one that held Duncan Henderson and his wife. She gazed at the passing scenery, amazed that for long stretches there were no houses visible. Slaves still working the fields paused to view the passing parade through the clouds of dust that followed their wake, then bent once more to their tasks. Tomorrow would be their celebration, the masters having given them the day off. Already some had prepared their huts and yards with some of the leftover lime that was used to whitewash the tree roots. Ginger root was boiled and sweetened with molasses or wet sugar. And the rum, their escape from the pain, awaited them.

It seemed an interminably long time before they arrived at McDowell's estate and Felice stood in awe as she alighted from the coach and was helped down by a footman from the McDowell estate. Samson rode away to hitch the carriage. Ahead of her, her father and his wife exited their carriage. Mary Henderson brushed at her gown; her husband stood stiffly next to her.

The magnificent white walled house stood on a slight incline and seemed to glow; its two stories to Felice appeared to reach up to the very sky. The entrance was a divided staircase with tall columns that made the Great House look even higher.

Inside, the floors were highly polished mahogany and Felice could imagine how many house servants it took with their coconut brushes and wax to get them this shiny. Crystal chandeliers with candles sparkled from the high ceiling. The place was all aglow with additional lighting from wall sconces.

Was this where Mulatto John lived? Felice gazed around, her head seeming to spin all the way on her neck as she tried to take it all in. She recalled the first time she was brought to her new room as a little child and everything looked too big for her alone. She felt a smallness while at the same time a feeling of self-assuredness engulfed her. She was at the ball with white people and there were many others who looked like her; mulattos who had powdered themselves white. They were mixing in and one had to look closely in some instances to know who was who. Here, it seemed, everybody was one and the same.

Liveried servants stood around the hallway, waiting to serve. Someone came up to Felice, extending an arm.

"Mulatto John!" she exclaimed.

"Just John," he corrected as he placed her hand in the crook of his arm, a smile on his lips.

He was dashing in his long coat and waistcoat, a cravat at his throat; more handsome than she recalled. Felice searched his eyes.

"John. How have you been?"

"I have survived. Come, let's join the merry crowd."

He whisked Felice away and into the ballroom where an orchestra played. Men and women danced together across the polished floor and everywhere people were engaged in conversation. Women flitted about, noses held high and men stood, hands behind their backs, and engaged in discussions, most likely about conditions in the colony. The scent of tobacco was thick in the room. Duncan Henderson and his wife were being introduced all around, Felice having been forgotten.

Mary Henderson seemed a different person as she smiled and flirted. Maybe she had been locked away for too long in her quarters and had forgotten that she had at one time been a social creature. She seemed almost alive as if, finally, she was among her peers.

"Would you care to dance?" John asked.

"I don't know how to," Felice responded.

"Then, I will teach you."

"I am an awful learner."

"We shall see about that. Just follow my lead."

With that, he led her away and onto the floor. She stood stiffly, awaiting his instructions. It wasn't hard for Felice to follow John's lead as he taught her the steps to the dance. What was hard was to keep her heart from beating too hard in her chest. Their bodies did not touch but her hand enfolded in his felt warm and safe.

"So, what has Felice Henderson been doing since I saw her last?" he questioned once he was sure she caught the rhythm.

"I kept wondering why I hadn't seen you. Is something wrong?"

"No, no. My father kept me confined due to all the disturbances occurring across the island. He feared for my safety."

"I see. So, this is where you live?"

"Yes. And someday it will all be mine."

There was a sudden pause in the music and a white man dressed in coat frock and tails and a powdered wig appeared at the entrance to the room, a wand in his hand and an air of showmanship in his demeanor.

"Ladies and Gentlemen. If I could have your attention, please? It is my pleasure to introduce to you this evening the celebrated Mr. Hyman Saunders."

There was general silence as the partygoers wanted to determine of what importance this man who had interrupted their enjoyment could be. John pulled Felice's arm closer to his body as if anchoring her to himself. He appeared excited at the prospect of the final revelation of the evening's best-kept secret.

"Mr. Saunders, recently returned from his travels in Europe and America, wishes to acquaint you with his dexterity in the art of conjuring," the man continued.

John dragged Felice to the front as the crowd gathered around the celebrated prestidigitator. The revelers were not disappointed at the exhibition as the man pulled his shirt off without removing his waistcoat, and fried German pancakes in the hats of his volunteers. Felice stood, her mouth agape as Saunders delivered as he had promised, offering to teach his skills to anyone willing to pay for the service. Not a few gathered around him to make appointments for private showings at their houses.

"Do you believe these are just tricks?" Felice asked of John as the show concluded.

"Most likely," John responded as he guided Felice out of the ballroom and to the cool air outside.

The yard was filled with carriages and servants standing guard. How easy it would be to start an uprising at this moment, Felice thought. The white people in their revelry would not notice until it was too late.

They were all gathered in one place and would soon be too drunk on the rum or rum punch to notice anything amiss. Goodness, she was thinking like a slave. Felice shook herself and walked down the steps with John.

No one looked at them, or if they did, pretended not to see them as they walked toward a grove of trees in the garden. He seated her on a rough bench. The darkness of the night engulfed them, the light of the moon easing its thickness somewhat so they could see each other's expressions.

"I missed riding with you, "John said into the stillness.

"I thought you had gone away again."

"No, my dear. My formal education is done. I am now being trained to manage the estate."

"It is huge," Felice ventured. "How will you manage?"

"There are overseers who do most of the managing. Fortunately, I have been paying attention to my father. He always took me along, ever since I was a child."

"Does he have any other children?"

"As far as I know I am the only one."

"What about your mother?"

"She has managed the household all my life. She is his wife for all intents and purposes."

"Is she here?"

"Yes. I will introduce you. Can we go riding again sometime?" he suddenly asked.

"I would love that."

"You look exceptionally beautiful tonight, Felice," John whispered.

"Thank you."

"I would like to ask your father's permission to call on you."

Felice sat silent and her eyes widened.

"Me?"

Her heart fluttered in her chest.

"Yes, my dear. You have become one beautiful woman and soon all the men will be rushing to your father's door. Some with the good intentions of making you their mistress. You are, right now, what they call a good catch."

"I don't know what to say."

"You like me, don't you, Felice?"

"Yes. Yes, I do."

"And what are your prospects as a mulatto woman in the colony?"

"I..."

"Exactly. I like you very much, Felice. I have thought of no one else ever since I met you."

Felice looked up into his eyes. They seemed to twinkle in the moonlight and her heart was racing. Suddenly, his face was blocking her view of the moon and his head was coming down to hers. Felice felt herself stiffen for a moment. Then his lips were upon hers. First, it was a quick taste before he lifted his head to gaze down into her eyes. Then they descended again for a deeper savoring. Felice felt her breath stop and then became aware that her heart was racing in her chest.

There was a sweetness about tasting his lips and, with his breath on her face, Felice felt this surely was what heaven must feel like. Her body grew warm. John pulled away and smiled down at her.

"Should we go back inside?" he asked, clearing his throat and rising to his full height.

Extending a hand, he pulled her up to stand in front of him. Felice felt somewhat unsteady on her feet. He smiled down at her and, tucking her hand in the crook of his arm, led her back to the house.

The dining room table was laden with more food than Felice had ever seen. Cook would have gone mad preparing such a spread.

There was seafood including mullet and snapper, meats like wild boar and turtle, and yams and vegetables with the side tables further burdened with cakes, puddings, and other desserts. And the rum flowed. For the faint of heart and the uninitiated there was Sangaree and Honey Dram with just a taste of rum.

Presiding over the table was a tall mulatto woman whose grace and elegance instantly identified her as the lady of the house. Her thick, black, wavy hair was pinned up on the top of her head accentuating her thin narrow face and straight nose. She was a handsome woman who bore an almost haughty expression and stance. The smooth skin of her face, however, refused to be lightened by powder, lack of sunlight, or any cosmetic made for that purpose. She would never pass for a white woman.

John was walking Felice over to her and the girl knew a moment of panic. Her heart still fluttered in her bosom from a few moments ago and the kiss she and John had shared. Now, to meet his mother! Her heart needed to slow down its pace first.

"Wait!" she whispered loudly once she recognized his intention.

But she was too late. They were already within view and the woman looked up to where her son was approaching her, a young girl in tow. Her eyes darted from one to the other, the smile she had prepared for her son now fading. Walking up to her, John planted a kiss on his mother's cheek.

"Mother, I would like you to meet Felice from Mr. Henderson's Greenrock," he introduced.

"Pleased to meet you, ma'am," Felice said with a deep curtsy.

The woman inclined her head but her solemn expression did not change. Felice felt the need to shuffle her feet and get as far away from this woman as possible. It was not the deep hatred she experienced from Mary Henderson; it was the disdain of "how dare you?" She wanted to run and hide but John held her fast at his side.

"She is Mr. Henderson's daughter," John explained further.

The woman's eyebrows raised a fraction and she attempted a smile.

"How are you, my dear?" she forced out.

"Well, thank you, ma'am."

Felice was not sure if she was to call her Mrs. McDowell. John had not indicated that his parents were married to each other. She was his slave wife she knew, but that did not mean that she was to be called Mrs. McDowell. Just like with Felice's own mother and father, the practice was for a man, even when married, to have another who acted as his wife. Some wives just had to accept the way it was. In John's case, there was no official Mrs. McDowell.

"I hope John is taking care of you?"

"Yes, he is," Felice said a bit breathlessly.

"Well, there is plenty of food. Eat as much as you want."

"Yes, ma'am."

Felice curtsied once more, realizing that she had just been dismissed. She felt tears beginning to form as she turned away. Cook's scowl flashed across her vision and she immediately straightened her back, held her head up, and forced the tears back to where they had come from.

How dare her? Who did she think she was? Felice felt an anger roil inside her. They were both the same class. What made her think she could behave that way toward her? She could take insolence from her father's wife; but not from this woman who was only a slave wife.

"Your mother does not like me," Felice gritted the moment she and John were out of earshot.

"She just has to get used to you," John comforted. "Do you want to eat or shall we dance?"

"I just want to crawl into the floor at this moment," Felice groaned.

"Felice, come. You will feel better with something in your stomach. What do you want to eat?"

"Nothing. I'm sorry, John."

"Come. Let's dance then."

Placing his hand at her elbow, he led her back to the ballroom.

Her father was just leaving the room, a tall but corpulent white man with a large stick of tobacco in his mouth at his side.

"Felice," Henderson called as she passed by. "I was wondering where the devil you had got to. Mr. Evan wishes to dance with you, my dear."

A terrified look crossed Felice's face as she glanced at John. Her father had successfully placed himself between the young people, his back to John.

"But I…" Felice protested.

"He won't bite you!" Henderson almost bellowed. "Welshmen seldom do," he continued with a chuckle.

John's face changed many colors but he remained mute, his hands crossed in front of him as if holding onto each other for support. In that moment he looked like a little lost boy about to cry.

"Excuse me, boy," Evan said as he grabbed onto Felice's elbow and guided her back to the ballroom.

Felice glanced over her shoulder but John had his head down. Henderson patted him on the back and returned to join the revelers.

Evan pulled Felice along and she felt she must surely fall flat on her face before he finally stopped in the middle of the dance floor. The scent of stale tobacco and a body not properly washed filled her nostrils. She thought of the sweet freshness of young John and how it had felt to have his hands enclose hers. Mr. Evan's girth was supposed to keep her at a distance; but with each move he made he rubbed against her. Felice felt her stomach turn and wondered when her torture would be over.

It was some time before she got her relief when John's father claimed her for a dance. Evan could not refuse his host. At least she was somewhat used to Mr. McDowell so it was not so bad; he was John's father, after all. Dancing with this strange man who looked to be even older than her father was the worst form of torture a young girl could ever know. She was grateful to John's father for rescuing her. After one dance, McDowell turned her over to John. The joy that thrilled through her body was more than she could have imagined. John whispered in her ear.

"I will not let you go again."

Felice felt him pull her close. She knew her father must not be pleased at what had just occurred but he could not very well insult his host and friend, even if his son was only the child of his mistress and little more than a slave.

The Christmas spirits flowed well that night and it was almost Christmas morning before Felice returned home. The cocks were crowing afar off and a donkey brayed in the interval. She was exhausted but her eyes were bright and alive. Her heart beat wildly in her chest. The sweetness of their stolen kiss lingered on her lips and caused waves of warmth to go through her body at the memory.

Their second kiss had lingered and drawn heat from both their bodies, threatening to consume them in one sweet swell. Felice had felt a pulsing in a part of her body she had not been aware could do that. They had snuck outside again when they realized that people were beginning to go home. They had to be together at least one more time because they were not sure when they would be able to see each other again. No one was about except for the drivers who waited patiently for their masters and mistresses. Felice almost bumped into Samson who quickly bowed and begged her excuse. The darkness of the night engulfed them and they seemed to blend into one.

How could something be so sweet, Felice asked herself as she sat in the carriage staring out at the darkness on her ride back home? Now she knew why men and women would sneak off when the Busha or Driver was not looking. It was like magic had been created between them. Now she understood the giggles she and Morgie would encounter as they roamed the bushes only to discover a man and woman wrapped around each other. She wondered if Morgie had ever experienced this; maybe with Samson. She must tell Morgie about this.

Felice could hear the *goombay* drums from a distance as they rode toward the estate. She could well imagine the revelers having a dance so different from the one she had just attended. There was no sleep that night for anyone on the estate, slave or free. Their bellies full with extra meat and wine given to them by their master, their pockets heavy with monies from sales of goods and services all that week before, the merrymakers were having a true *bacchanal*.

Christmas morning Felice awoke to music and dance performed by the slaves on the estate as they headed toward the Great House. She had not got much sleep as she had lain awake for a long time thinking about the evening that had just passed. How could she sleep when thoughts of John and how he had held her swirled around her head?

Wearing masks and carrying wooden swords, the revelers pranced in the air and beat their drums, recalling another place and another time when they were free, body and soul.

The women behind them, drunk from last night's revelries plied the performers with aniseed water. This was the time of the year that Felice loved best. It was as if everyone had forgotten their status and celebrated together.

Mr. Henderson lay out a spread and the slaves moved in and out of the Great House, taking care to tread lightly because they knew how hard they themselves had worked to cook the food and clean the house. They knew that it was the sweat of their brow and the bending to almost breaking of their backs in the broiling heat that had provided the feast that now lay on the table in the dining room.

As a child, Felice had been afraid of the performers and their grotesque masks: the huge house on someone's head, the horsehead, the cow-head, and devil. Hiding behind Cook's skirt with Morgie, she had peeked out at the masqueraders in their colorful clothes leaping high into the air with their wooden swords and shouting 'John Connu'. Their performances came from a place they were trying to recall; their dress a mimicry of the place their master had not forgotten but held dear to his bosom as a better place than this.

Felice walked over to where her sister sat on a stone in the yard with Samson next to her, shoveling food into his mouth. He had been one of the men prancing in his mask but now his head was bare, his body still clothed in the pitchy-patchy garment that was his costume. Morgie was dressed in a blue gown. She was one of the set girls who competed with the other set of women dressed in red to see who was better in song, dance, and dress. They had worked all year on their dresses and performances. Later, they would all take to the streets and go from house to house, performing and hoping to get food and money from their neighbors. All the way from the eve of Christmas to the first of the New Year was their time. When all this was over, the Massa would take back his time and the enslaved would return to their normal position of labor and toil; what they were told was their lot.

"You enjoying youself, Miss Felice?" Morgiana asked as her sister approached them.

"Yes, Morgie. Very much," Felice assured.

"We going walk afta dis."

"I know. I wish I could join you."

"You always did like di Jankanu. Remember how we use to run unda di bed an hide from cow-head?"

Felice chuckled at the memory. How could she be angry at her sister? She was the only one she could talk to who did not treat her as if she was better than or less than. Morgie could not very well refuse to talk to her anyway; at least not in public. She glanced across to where Cook sat on a chair in all her glory as Queen, *maam* of the festivities. The woman Mino of the Popo country stood next to her dressed in an old gown whose length appeared a little too short for her. She was, indeed an amazon of a woman. Her eyes connected with Felice's and the woman nodded at her in recognition, her face still set as if she was ready for fight. Felice still could not help the shiver that ran down her spine as their eyes connected. The women of the Popo country were dangerous women, she had heard.

Quaco stood in warrior costume, his eyes now bright with fight as if he had somehow been transported back to his homeland. His wife Mary looked uncomfortable next to him in a hand-me-down from her mistress to which she had added her own touches of color. Perhaps she would be more comfortable in the dress of her homeland too like her husband. But that would not do in a land such as this. A woman, even though a slave, should not be a warrior or appear as a savage. How could a white man *cum* such a woman? It would be akin to coupling with a beast.

It was acceptable for a man, after all, it was only a show, a performance which the whites chuckled at while they drank the white rum, amused at the antics of the men jumping over sticks and dancing themselves into a frenzy as they chanted gibberish. The woman, like every other woman, should dress in petticoat and gown and walk with a parasol to shade her from the sun, if only this one time. Her skin would never lighten anyway, sun or not. A woman should always appear as a woman.

As Felice watched the group rise as if on signal, she felt a moment of longing. Samson replaced his mask with Morgiana's help. Cook, her cow-skin whip in hand, assumed her role as Queen or *maam* with Mino by her side. And the cacophony of the *goombay* and other instruments they made or found began. Their sounds reverberated in the air long after they were gone.

The Master's Daughter   Vjange Hazle

CHAPTER 7

Duncan Henderson's estate quietened down as the morning sun rose on the second day of the year 1777. He had not lost any of his slaves during the freedom of the previous week but some of the neighboring planters had. With everyone drunk and carefree, some slaves found it an opportune time to make their escape, either to join the Maroons and other rebels or to head for the capital of the island and claim they were free men or women. The *Cornwall Chronicle* had frequent lists of the runaways as well as the newly arrived. Lucky for him his stock was steady except for a few deaths from old age or some other unavoidable disease common to the tropics earlier in the year. He had an increase of seven due to births. He could only hope they survived their first year of life and grew to be strong and healthy. He believed treating his slaves well could only result in high returns. So far, so good.

What Duncan Henderson was not privy to was the 'mashing up' of the House headdress in the all night ceremony that took place before the slaves returned to work. The *myal*-man destroyed the John Connu house, which was the headdress of the leader during the dances. Its symbolism would probably have been lost on the man who was content that he treated his slaves better than most. Whippings were almost unheard of on his estate and any necessary punishment was meted out fairly. Not like one of his planter friends who dished out the disgusting Derby's dose more often than necessary.

The celebrations were over until later in the year when they would begin their preparations again for the festivities that meant for them a few days to feel freedom in their bodies, even this once in the year. It was as free as they could hope to be except for funerals and sometimes marriages of some who were free people of color when the Massa allowed them to beat the drums as long as they wished; as long as they were fit and ready for work the next day.

Henderson looked up as Felice entered the study.

"You want to see me, Massa Henderson?" Felice asked in the most cultivated voice she could muster.

Henderson cleared his throat noisily as he looked his daughter over.

"Yes. Sit, will you?"

Felice did her father's bidding and sat primly on the edge of an armchair across from his desk. Miss Rutherfurd had taught her well.

"Are you well?" he asked, looking intently at her from beneath his bushy eyebrows.

"Yes, sir."

"Good. I have a proposal for you. You know what a proposal is, don't you?"

"Yes, sir."

"Do you recall a Mr. Evan?"

It was all Felice could do to keep her face from wrinkling in disgust. Memories of his scent swirled around her brain. She swallowed before responding.

"Yes, sir."

"Well, dear Felice, it appears my friend has taken a fancy to you," he said, a note of contentment in his tone as he laced his fingers together on the desk.

"What?"

Felice almost shot to the floor in a most unladylike fashion; but she had learned very well from Miss Rutherfurd. So she sat with a stoic face and eyebrows raised just so, her voice just almost imperceptibly higher.

"Calm down, dear girl. It is not that bad. Mr. Evan would like to take care of you, it seems."

"Take care of me, sir? But I am alright here. I don't need to be taken care of."

Henderson cleared his throat uncomfortably.

"How must I explain this to you, Felice? My friend would like to take you on as his mistress."

"Mistress? Whatever do you mean? As in marriage?"

Henderson uttered a loud guffaw, which made his whiskers

shake.

"Marriage? Felice, dear child, a white man does not marry a mulatto in this land. He simply keeps her as his woman. He cannot risk being fined or imprisoned. Now, my dear, Evan is willing to provide you with a house and a bit of land of your own. In exchange you are to be his mistress and belong to no other."

Felice sat in a daze. Be Evan's mistress? Her stomach churned; her mind was in turmoil. John. He was offering to court her. Had he already spoken with her father? How could she tell her father that she much preferred the young and handsome John who made her body quiver and that she longed for his touch in the deep night when she curled herself under the sheets? How could she tell him she longed to ride with him again and feel the movement of his body against hers and his sweet breath on the back of her neck?

"But, I don't want to be anyone's mistress," Felice protested when she finally found her voice. "I am quite content here."

"Felice, you cannot remain here forever. You are coming of age now and must take your part in the world. This is the perfect solution to our problem."

Felice was silent. She had not known there was a problem. She must see John.

"Does my mother know about this, sir?"

"Isabella has no say in this. *She* cannot provide for you. You cannot work as a slave or anything else for that matter. This is the right thing to do."

"Please, sir. I rather become a shopkeeper than be mistress to an old man I do not know."

"What?" Henderson bellowed. "You dare?"

"If you please, sir, give me a shop to keep. We could import items from England. I will give you some of my profits, whatever you agree to, but I will not be this man's mistress."

"Felice, listen to me. You have no choice in the matter."

She would rather drown herself in the Great River than have that man touch her. How could her father do this to her? There were mulattos on the island whose fathers had given them businesses to run. Montego Bay, the old Lard Bay, was fast becoming a center of commerce. She knew she could do it, she just knew it.

And, having felt the youthful touch of Mulatto John, she could not imagine being touched by anyone else. She would die first before she allowed other hands to rove across her body. She had to speak with Cook. The woman would not agree to it, she was sure. Her silence must have indicated to her father that Felice had consented to his commands. Dismissing her, he returned to his perusal of the *Cornwall Chronicle*. The Hibberts, Montagues, and Bernards had recent shipments of slaves from the Gold Coast. Well, bully for them.

Felice hurried to the cookhouse. She could hear Cook humming a tune as she stirred the three-foot pot of soup on the open fire. Morgiana was peeling the foodstuff to be placed in the pot. They both looked up as Felice entered. Cook paused to study the face of her child.

"What wrong, Felice?" she asked sharply.

"Missa Henderson talk to you yet?" Felice asked in the native tongue.

"No. What happen?"

"You woulda nevah believe dis…"

"Felice, talk proper!" Cook commanded.

"Missa Henderson want me to be mistress to one a him old friend."

"Felice, what yuh saying to me?"

"A stinking old man name Evan."

"Say dat again," Cook pleaded.

"I just come from the study. Him tell me Missa Evan interested in me. I ask him if is for marriage him say no, white man doan marry mulatto."

Cook was silent. She had paused in her stirring of the pot but now turned again to her task.

"Felice, listen to yuh fadda," Cook finally advised.

"What?"

"Listen to Missa Henderson."

"I can't believe this. You want me to be mistress to some old and smelly white man?"

"Is not what I want dat matter, Felice. Is for di best."

Felice stared at her mother and then at her sister. Morgiana looked away.

"I cannot believe this. I thought you loved me."

"Love? I love you enough. But is what is best fi yuh. Who gwine married to you, Felice? White man cyaant. Nigga man cyaant tek care a yuh for no matta how him free him can nevah have enough money. Mulatta man a look fi white woman from England. Yuh got gold spoon in yuh mouth right now. Tek it an use it."

Felice felt in that moment like she had been slapped and rejected. She could not believe her mother was doing this to her. She wanted to tell her about John. She wanted to let her know that a man, a man white by law, was ready to court her and make her his wife. But she was not sure if he had himself been rejected by her father and even now was searching elsewhere for a wife whose father was willing to give his consent. Turning on her heels, Felice wheeled out of the cookhouse and hurried back to the house and toward her room, tears almost blinding her.

"Where are you off to in such a hurry?"

Mary Henderson stood in the hallway blocking Felice's progress toward the stairs. The woman had been ill and had shed some pounds because she could not eat much solid food without bringing it back up. The doctor was still unsure of what was wrong with her but it was a good thing that she was no longer rolling around the estate trying to fit into her old gowns. Aquila stood behind her with a smirk on her face.

"To my room, Missis," Felice responded with a curtsy and attempted to walk by her.

"Your days here are numbered, you know that? I have had Mr. Henderson take care of you, you…you…"

Felice gazed at the woman who stood before her, a self-satisfied smile on her face.

"What do you mean by that?" the girl demanded.

"Just that. Now show some respect and get out of my sight. You make me sick to my stomach."

Felice stood for a moment. Then, gathering her skirts, she pushed pass the shocked woman and marched up the stairs.

"But see here!" Aquila exclaimed at her retreating back.

"Don't worry, Aquila. She will be gone from here soon."

Felice was shaking and her fingers could barely grasp the handle of the door to her room. She boiled with anger as she flung herself onto her bed. Enough of this! Enough of being shoved aside like an unwanted mongrel. She must find Mulatto John. She must know if he had been able to speak to her father.

Later, as dusk fell, Felice, a small bag across her shoulder, crept from the Great House and headed toward the slave quarters. As she approached the hut Samson shared with his mother and father, a dark figure detached itself from the doorway. It seemed he had been waiting for her and knew what she wanted.

"Take me to the McDowell's," Felice whispered in the gathering darkness.

He did not respond but walked off. Felice followed behind, trying to keep up with his long strides. A small old carriage awaited them in the carriage house and Felice wondered if he always kept a carriage at the ready. It was smaller than the one she had ridden in to the party at Christmas. Samson helped her in.

Felice sat on the rough wooden seat of the carriage. It was one they often used to carry supplies to the *barcadier* to ship goods by canoe downriver that were easier transported by water than by land. It was uncomfortable to say the least; but at the moment her comfort was not part of her thought. She hoped to God that John was at home. Otherwise, she was willing to wait in the bushes until she could see him. But she was not going back to that place. She did not know how John would receive her but it could not be worse than this.

She knew Samson was taking a chance helping her on her

journey. If they were stopped, he could be killed right away, especially with a mulatto woman, his master's daughter in his carriage. He was not a free man to roam about as he pleased or without a ticket; and with his master's vehicle? He risked a death sentence and Felice worried all the way until the dark Great House came into view. Samson stopped before the long driveway.

"Miss Felice, I sorry but I cyaant tek you any further," he said as he opened the door.

"I understand. Thank you, Samson," she responded, handing him a handkerchief in which she had wrapped a few coins.

"Is awright, Miss Felice. You might need it more dan me."

Felice was unsure what his words meant. He returned to his seat on the carriage and rode off, leaving her standing in the dark night with only nature's creatures for company. She stood for a moment glancing around her, wondering what she had done.

A slight chill was in the air and the darkness seemed to sit heavy on her. She could make out the shapes of the trees and this was where she headed. How would she find John? She had not thought about that in making her plans. She did not know where his room was. She could be waiting for days until she caught sight of him and risked being spotted by workers as they went about their daily business. They might say nothing; after all, what business was it of theirs that the mulatto daughter of a white planter felt it better to roll about like a rolling calf on the plantation than to remain in the comfort of the Great House, even if it did not belong to her or her to it?

Felice walked between the trees, her eyes darting around at the shadows. She could not risk being seen by the watchmen as she walked up the driveway and she could not very well walk up to the front door and knock and ask if John was in. The cool air filled her nostrils with the scent of the cedar trees. Unsure of what she should do next, she walked around the house, hoping that somewhere there might be a light in someone's window and she would know for sure that someone was at home, even if it was not John.

There was an eeriness about the house as all activity had ceased for the night. The slaves were in their quarters a good distance from the house trying to rest their weary bodies after a long day's toil and would rise all too soon to begin again when morning light came. Many had not washed before laying their bodies down, the scent and stain of the soil heavy on their skins. Some had not even changed the ragged clothing they wore, even if they had received new clothing at Christmas. Their massa had given them mackerel, rum, and sugar, and their yearly supply of *oznaburg*; but they would have to wait to get those sewn into trousers and shirts and frocks they would wear for the whole of the next year. In the meantime they would wear these old ones some more until they fell from their bodies. Some had received clothing, quite likely the Massa and his family's castoffs. Those too, would have to wait for another time.

The sound of a horse's hooves reached Felice's ears and she quickly slipped behind a tree, hoping she had not been too late. The shiny black animal flew by, its nostril flaring. Its rider's shirt was white against the darkness. John.

He was gone before Felice could stop him and for a moment, she wondered if she had only dreamed him up. Instinctively, she ran after the animal, hoping she would somehow catch up with him; but it was to no avail. The horse and its rider disappeared into the black night. Felice leaned against a tree, breathless. Then she slid down its length and sat on the ground.

What had she done? What had she been thinking? She should have waited until light of day and inquired about him; maybe send Samson with a message. There must be a way to send a message to him; the slaves sent messages across plantations to each other all the time as they plotted their rebellions. How foolish she had been to think she could just arrive in the dark of night and he would magically appear as if he had been waiting for her.

The cold, dark, and lonely night stretched ahead of her. If only she had asked Samson to wait for her. She hoped he was not going to be in any trouble. The thought of him being whipped for helping her to escape was hard to bear. Morgie would hate her forever.

Cook was going to be furious at her. But *Felice* was furious at her mother. How could she even think to have her be mistress of someone like Evan? Maybe Cook had never seen the man himself. Felice was sure even Cook would refuse to be with such a man with his red and blotchy face and extended belly; he was old enough to be her father, for God's sake.

Her father, Duncan Henderson, was a handsome man who took care of himself, unlike so many of the other planters, and Felice could only imagine what he must have looked like as a young man. She could well imagine young Isabella getting together with Duncan Henderson. They must have loved each other very much; even now they were still together, despite his wife now being part of the household. Cook and Morgie still shared the small room in the house; he had not thrown her out when his family arrived. He must care a good deal about her, Felice concluded.

The sound of a horse's canter awoke her from her musings and Felice quickly jumped up as the animal approached. Brutus shied and John held firmly to the reins as he tried to quieten the animal with low murmurs and pats to the side of its neck. The animal pranced nervously until it settled down to John's whispers and touch. Sliding off Brutus' back, John landed on his feet in front of Felice.

"Felice?" he whispered uncertainly.

"Hello, John," Felice responded, thinking how ghastly she must look with her hair falling down and her clothing in disarray.

"What are you doing here?"

"I'm sorry. I shouldn't have come."

Felice felt as if tears were forming and she quickly blinked them back.

"Whatever is the matter?"

"I should go back to Greenrock. I made a horrible mistake."

"Is everything alright, Felice?"

"No, John. But it is not your problem. I will return to my father's plantation. I shouldn't have come. Really."

"Felice, it is late. Come inside where we can talk."

"Are you sure it is alright?"

"Yes. Everyone has gone to bed. Come."

Leading her by the elbow and his horse by the reins, John walked toward the stable. The scent of the stables was strong in the night air and Felice could hear the snorts of the other animals from within. After leading the horse inside and closing the door behind him, John turned to her.

"Are you hungry?"

"No."

Although she had eaten earlier in the evening, Felice could feel the beginnings of her hunger since it was so long ago; but she refused to let him know. It was enough that she had come uninvited in the darkness of the night. There was so much she had not thought about when she had hurriedly made her plans to leave home.

In silence, he led her to a door at the side of the house and let himself in. It was dark inside except for a candle that burned in the hallway, casting a soft glow around the room. Picking up the holder, he guided her up the wide staircase to a landing, cautioning her to walk on tiptoe. He paused in front of a room door and turned the doorknob. Felice realized that this must be John's quarters.

The bed in the center of the room was a large canopied mahogany that looked like it was built for a king. Mr. McDowell took care of his only son, it seemed. Her father had done his best to see to her comfort; but it was nothing like the luxury in which McDowell's mulatto son lived. Felice looked away from the bed and glanced around the rest of the richly furnished room. John led her to a chair that was in front of a writing desk on one side of the large room. All around were books with titles she had never seen before. Felice sat facing him.

"Are you sure I cannot get you something to eat?" John asked from where he leaned against a large mahogany gentleman's clothes press.

"No. I will be alright," she reassured as she quelled the twinges in her belly.

"Whatever happened?" he finally asked his eyes boring into hers for an answer.

"Have you had a chance to speak with my father?" Felice inquired, trying to meet his gaze but feeling a shyness inside.

"No. I spoke with my father and he promised to make the arrangements for me to meet with your father. I don't think he quite got around to it yet. Why, may I ask?"

"My father has arranged for me to be mistress to Mr. Evan."

"You don't say. Should I ask how you feel about that?" he asked in a deceptively soft tone.

Felice looked at him. His eyes were searching hers as if for reassurance.

"I am here," Felice responded.

John was silent as he digested her news. Placing his hands in the pockets of his trousers he looked up at the ceiling as if for an answer and then let out a slow breath which caused his lips to pout somewhat. Then he began slowly pacing the room, his brow furrowed. It was awhile before he spoke again.

"It is late. Why don't we sleep on this and I will speak with my father in the morning."

"Alright. But where will I sleep?"

"You, my dear, may sleep in my bed. I will make *my* bed on the floor."

"Are you sure now? I don't wish to put you out."

"Don't you worry about it. Now, let us get some rest so we can think about this more clearly in the morning. Come."

Removing her bag from across her shoulder, he led Felice to his bed.

"Do you have a nightgown in which to sleep?"

"No, I did not think of that. I am sorry, John. I really should go back to my father's. I really should not have bothered you. I don't know what I was thinking."

"Felice, stop. It is my problem too. I told you I wish to court you and if there is someone else in the way then I have a problem. Like I said, let's get some rest. I will give you one of my shirts to sleep in."

Felice smiled up at him. His eyes darkened and a certain tenderness came over his face. For a moment, she thought that he would kiss her and, for a moment, she *hoped* he would. The memory of their kisses was still strong. It just felt so safe being there with him and hear him say they would deal with it in the morning. She was no longer alone. John would stand with her on this.

Pulling out a shirt from the wardrobe, he handed it to her with a smile.

"I will turn my back while you change," he promised with a grin.

Felice felt conscious of herself as she removed her dress and pulled the shirt over her head. It seemed to swallow her whole body and she rolled the sleeves up so they would not hang over her fingers. His clothes smelled fresh and clean as if only the best imported soap had been used to launder it. She pulled away the covers and slipped between the sheets. He had stayed true to his word and had kept his back turned.

"Is it safe now?" he asked, a smile sounding in his tone.

"Yes," she responded as she pulled the covers up to her chin.

The sheets were not the rough ones Felice was used to but seemed to be of the finest linen. John was a fortunate one. Her sheets, though of linen, were not the best and were rough on her skin. But who was she to complain? When she thought of how Morgiana, even her mother, lived she was glad her father had made the decision to take care of her. Too many had not been so fortunate.

"Goodnight, Felice," John whispered as he blew out the candle and lowered himself onto the floor.

Felice felt bad that she had forced him to sleep on the floor. If only she had not come. But how else would she have been able to speak to him? By now, she probably would have been sent off to Evan's house or wherever he planned to set her up as his mistress. He probably would want to give her a house for herself if he had a wife. Many of the plantation owners in the colony practiced that habit. Some of the wives knew but had no choice but to accept that their husbands were keeping another woman, most likely a mulatto, as if she were his wife.

She could hear every movement John made and with each move she felt worse. He was not used to sleeping on such a hard surface. Poor thing. She would gladly switch places with him but did not know how to suggest it. Finally, she heard him rise and sit up.

"Are you alright?" Felice whispered.

"I will be. I will sleep in my Aunt Ethel's room, if you don't mind."

"I am sorry, John. You are not used to sleeping like this. I will gladly trade places with you."

"I will be alright, my dear. It is not easy for me to sleep with you so close by. Goodnight, my dear. I will be in the room down the hall."

She heard him rise and then the closing of the door.

The darkness seemed thicker and the room more silent after John left and Felice shuffled down some more under the covers. His scent enveloped her and she inhaled deeply. It would be nice if he was right next to her to make her feel safe. Her body grew warm at the thought of being held close to his body all night.

The morning light was creeping into the room when Felice finally fell asleep. She had lain awake listening to the sounds of the night coming through the window wondering if they had yet missed her back home. She hoped Samson was alright and that he had not got into any trouble for helping her escape.

A gasp startled Felice awake. In the middle of the room stood John's mother, a towel over an arm and a scowl on her forehead.

"What, in heaven's name, are you doing in my son's bed?" the woman demanded.

Felice sat upright, her mind unable to come up with an explanation.

"I'm so sorry, ma'am," she stammered, wrapping the covers across her chest.

"What have you done with my John?" she accused.

"He is in his aunt's room, ma'am," Felice tried to explain.

"How dare you."

"I can explain, ma'am."

"You need to get out at once."

The door opened and John entered, his hair ruffled and his clothes in disarray.

"Mother!" he exclaimed.

"What is this?" his mother demanded, pointing disdainfully at Felice.

"Mother, do you remember Mr. Henderson's Felice?"

"I know who she is. What is she doing in your bed?"

"She had nowhere to go, Mother, so I let her sleep in my room. No harm done."

"No harm done? Your father will be hearing about this."

"Please, Mother. We have to help her."

"What do you mean 'help her'?"

"I must speak with Father first. Felice, get dressed, will you, my dear? I will send Martha with some water for you to get cleaned up."

Hurriedly Felice grabbed her discarded clothes.

"John, whatever is going on here? I demand to know."

"Mother, let's allow Felice some privacy while she gets dressed. I will be back for you, my dear."

Felice nodded while he ushered his mother from the room and closed the door behind them. She had not meant to get him in trouble. What had she done? His father could send him away and leave him with nothing. Granted he was considered white by law and had more power than his mulatto mother. But his father was the one with the power of his life in his hands.

The room door opened again and a Negro woman entered. This must be Martha. The woman poured water into a white basin on a stand under the window and handed Felice a rag and a towel. Felice smiled her thanks and waited until she was alone before beginning to wash herself. Stripping herself of John's shirt, she began her abulations, her mind far away.

What awaited her this day? John's mother would surely oppose this union. His father would quite likely agree with their joining; *her* father might not. But the hatred John's mother displayed toward her was so thick it could be cut with a knife. Why did women hate her so? Mary Henderson would gladly poison her if she could and Aquila would gladly administer that poison. Mino, the Popo woman had no reason to dislike her as far as she knew; but the woman seemed like she would easily dispatch of Felice with a swift swing of her bill. The only women who seemed to care about her were her mother and Morgie and even then she sometimes wondered about her sister.

One moment Morgie was with her and another she was a warrior woman fighting to be free. The memory of the whipping Morgie had almost received not a year ago still made Felice cringe. How could two sisters live so differently: one a slave, the other free? Felice could not imagine being enslaved; although sometimes she wondered if she would not have been better off being bound. At least she would know her place.

The sound of movements outside the door jolted her from her musings. Hurriedly, Felice dressed. The only clothing she had brought with her was a change of underclothes. Hunger gnawed at her belly as a nervousness swept through her.

Maybe she should make her escape while she still could. Return to her father's estate and ask for forgiveness. She would agree to his terms and become the mistress of Evan. It could not be so bad; after all, what were her other choices? A shudder ran through her at the thought of his hands on her flesh.

Plenty of mulattos were destined for this fate. Caught in between, they could take only what was offered to them. Maybe it was just her lot. She thought of her mother and sister. Her mother had been born a slave and would perhaps die a slave; so had her sister Morgie, although Morgie was so determined to become free by joining the rebels.

So far, the island was quiet. There were whispers here and there of planned revolts but these had been quickly squelched. The Maroons were appearing in small groups every now and then, laying waste plantations across the island and striking fear in the hearts of whites. Their ability to disguise themselves in the landscape was particularly troubling. But, the uprisings were mostly on the other side of the island. Not only were they seeking vengeance, they were also seeking sustenance owing to the scarcity of food.

Felice herself had been protected from much of this. But Spanish ships were appearing in the waters as if sniffing out the possibilities for a recapture of the island. The talk was on the tongue of all the planters and their fear was real. What would happen to Felice should such an event occur?

Picking up her bag from off the floor where she had let it fall the night before, she slung it across her shoulders. She must get back to her father's house. She would not be treated like this by the likes of John's mother. Opening the door she came face to face with John.

"Felice, I was just coming to get you."

"I must get back, John."

"I just spoke with my father. He agrees that he will speak with your father about my intentions. Now, let us get you some food and then I will take you home."

Felice could almost hear her belly rumble as small pains gnawed at her. She wanted to be out of that house as soon as she could. She could not face John's mother across the table. But her hunger was calling to be satisfied.

She followed John down the stairs. His mother sat stone faced at the table and his father across from her. The table was laden with plates of cassava and fish and bowls of fruit. McDowell acknowledged Felice with a grunt and indicated for her to sit. John smiled at her as he pulled out a chair for her before claiming one next to her.

They ate mostly in silence with an occasional grunt of pleasure from John's father as he savored his meal. There was no mention of their dilemma and Felice felt herself begin to relax and enjoy the meal despite John's mother's scowls. Cook was by far the best cook in the world, she concluded. The fish and the cassava bread were not dry enough.

The meal over, John's mother rose and disappeared without

even a glance at Felice. A small carriage was brought around and John assisted Felice in before joining his father in an accompanying carriage. The small procession moved off, headed to Duncan Henderson's Greenrock.

Felice's heart fluttered in her chest.

The Master's Daughter   Vjange Hazle

CHAPTER 8

Mary Henderson lay pale and sallow in the middle of the huge mahogany four-poster bed in her room. Her uncombed hair was spread around her head on the pillow. She had been up all night, unable to sleep, catching a few nods in the armchair only to be awakened retching and in pain. The bags under her eyes hung heavy. Her chest heaved and she sat back up.

"Aquila, raise the pillow, will you?" she commanded in a raspy voice.

Aquila obeyed, lifting her mistress's head and placing an additional pillow behind it. She watched the woman close her eyes again. It had been a hard night sitting up watching the missis and cleaning up after her. This was not what she had expected when she was assigned as Mary Henderson's 'lady-in-waiting'. Wearing her mistress's castoffs had become more and more difficult as the woman began gaining weight and Aquila had had to use her seamstress skills to take in some of the dresses to make them fit. Now, the woman seemed to be shrinking as her illness began ravaging her body. Aquila was now afraid to wear the discarded clothes because no one knew what was wrong with Mary Henderson.

Dr. Bayly had been sent for but had not yet arrived, being away in Bluefields Bay and also attending to the Negroes on

Mr. Thistlewood's Breadnut Island Pen. He was coming to bleed Mary Henderson. She had been taking the mercury pills he had prescribed the last time he saw her; but her condition only seemed to worsen. The room door opened and Duncan Henderson entered, Felice behind him.

"What is *she* doing here?" Mary Henderson demanded, her pale brow furrowed.

Duncan Henderson did not respond to his wife's question.

"How are you feeling, my dear?" he inquired.

Felice was surprised at the tone of gentleness in her father's voice, especially given all that had occurred since she had returned home after having run away. She had never seen his face so red with anger and, were it not for John and his father standing on either side of her, she would have passed out from fear of the rage she saw in his eyes. The men had gone into the study while Felice was sent to her room.

Samson was in the bilboes after having confessed to helping Felice on her way. He had been flogged first and then fastened to the floor for one whole day. And Morgie refused to speak to Felice.

Cook found herself in Felice's room where the young girl lay across her bed looking up at the ceiling. She did not bother to knock before entering. The front of her dress was soiled with the food she had been preparing for lunch and she smelled of fish freshly caught.

"Why you do dat, Felice?" Cook demanded of her daughter.

"I do not owe you an explanation," Felice responded, refusing to even glance at her mother.

"Oh, so you turn big woman all of a sudden."

Felice did not respond, pretending there was no one else in the room.

"I want to tell you: be careful. Life not easy an half a bread betta dan no bread at all."

"Please leave," Felice said quietly.

"You gwaan. Chicken merry but hawk deh near, I tell you."

"Go away, will you?"

"Felice, listen to me. Missa Evan can give you more dan you can ever get in life. You is a malatta and nobody waan to married a malatta."

"Well, John does."

"What?"

"He is asking my father for my hand as we speak," Felice informed a smirk on her face as she turned to face Cook.

Cook stood aghast.

"Felice, you open your leg?" she asked fiercely.

"What do you mean?" Felice demanded, springing upright on the bed.

"Oh. How *you* so sure Mass John want to married you?" she asked suspiciously.

"Because he told me so," Felice responded smugly.

And so it was arranged and Felice Henderson and John McDowell were set to be married after a period of courtship like any proper English lady and gentleman. And then, Mary Henderson's health got worse and she became confined to her bed and their plans had to be shoved aside for a while. Mary Henderson's illness could not be diagnosed by Dr. Bayly, physician to both the enslaved and the free.

Felice looked at the pale face of the woman laying in the bed before her. Even in her illness, Mary Henderson was not ready to show Felice any kindness.

"Felice has expressed concern to me about the mercury pills you have been taking, my dear," Henderson continued, ignoring the scowl on his wife's face. "Could they possibly be the cause of your condition getting worse?"

"What does *she* know? Imbecile," Mary Henderson growled. "Get her out of my sight, will you?"

"Mary, my dear, I am inclined to agree with her somewhat. I am recommending that you stop taking them, at least for a while."

"Duncan, please. I have no time to listen to fairy tales and fantasies concocted in the mind of a half-wit. And, may I remind you that *you* are no physician?"

"Mary, Felice is no half-wit. She has just about as much education as any of her peers anywhere."

Aquila shifted from barefoot to barefoot where she stood next to the head of her mistress' bed. She cleared her throat.

"Do you have something to say, Aquila," her master addressed her.

"A-hm, yes, Massa. I tink dem might be obeah Miss Mary, sah."

"Ridiculous!" Henderson bellowed.

"No, Massa. It not ridicle."

"Preposterous! I refuse to listen to such nonsense."
"It not nonsense, Massa. An I know who do it."

"Pray. Tell me," he offered drily.

"Is Mino, sah."

"Who?"

"She from Popo, sah."

"Whatever do you mean, Aquila?"

"Well, Massa, Mino she come not too long an ever since is all kind of tings a happen. Look how Hamlet get blind an Mingo and him fambly get sick wid bellyache an vomiting. Worser, Ol' Pontiac just drop dung dead so? It cyaan be so-so so, Massa."

"Stop!" Henderson commanded. "All poppycock."

"Pappycack, Massa? Pompey was a man wid him own mare and see wha happen to him? Strong working mare kick ova dead, river wash way him house. How much calamity one man can get so, Massa? Is a warrior ooman, Massa, an a so she win war. If you doan believe me, Massa, look eena har hut."

Henderson's face was twisted in anger.

"What do you think, Felice?" he demanded, turning to his mulatto daughter.

Felice started.

"I..I am not sure, sir."

"Come on, young woman, you must have some opinion."

Felice pulled herself up. She was now a woman to be married. She would no longer be just the mulatto daughter of a white master. It was like her father was seeing her for the first time.

"Well, sir, I am not sure I understand how this obeah works but I do believe that your wife has a real issue that needs to be addressed."

There was an intake of breath from Aquila.

"Massa, you gwine lissen to a young bud dat doan know no storm rather dan lissen to a big ooman like me?"

Aquila hissed her teeth loudly.

"Be quiet, Aquila. Very diplomatic of you, Felice, but I will have someone check Mino's hut just to satisfy Aquila's concerns."

Aquila smirked at Felice. Felice looked through her. Soon she herself would be a Missis; after all, she was to be married to a man who was white by law. The likes of Aquila would be so far beneath her then. She will have to call her 'Missis'.

Mary Henderson suddenly rose to sit upright and Aquila grabbed an empty pail that stood next to the bed. Her missis retched into it and Aquila hurried out to dispose of the contents. The woman's brow was sweaty and her breathing was causing her chest to heave.

Quickly, Felice grabbed a rag and dipped it in a basin of water by the bed. She squeezed the excess water out and placed the rag on the woman's forehead. Mary Henderson's hand moved to brush away Felice's assistance but her husband's swift movement arrested her action. Felice mopped at the woman's brow. She could hear the raspy breathing.

Felice's reading and tutoring by Miss Rutherfurd had not been for nothing. From her perusal of medical books in the library she recognized that there was something seriously wrong with Mrs. Henderson's lungs. She did not need to be a physician to know that her condition was not the result of obeah. The climate had not been kind to Mary Henderson since her arrival; but she had been able to adjust as time passed. In fact, had she not preferred to spend her days lounging on her verandah being fanned and fed by the servants, she would have become one of the healthier white women in the colony. There were horses to ride and walks to take in the cool of evening. There were visits to be made to surrounding estates, plantations, and pens. There were excursions into Montego Bay and Bluefields Bay to enjoy the blue waters that were warm and welcoming to all.

The colony was not quite kind to the whites who came in search of their fortune in the new land. With yellow fever and malaria ever present, many were felled before they could become seasoned. Some had fled back to their homeland, cursing the colony they left behind them, penning journals and diaries that painted the place as a hotbed for disease and every form of debauchery known and as yet unknown to man. Others had fled and, while keeping their holdings in the colony, enriched themselves and found their way into the aristocracy of Europe.

It was not kind to the slaves either, or any other person who arrived, whether forced or voluntary; but, these could easily be replaced. It did not matter whether they lived or died. They would most likely not be able to return to the place from which they had come, anyway. Some, by then, had forgotten where that was anyway. Even if they did remember, how would they get there and make their way back to their village? For many, it had taken them days to cross the land to get to the ocean.

Mary Henderson's gaze toward where she knew the harbor must be was dimming though in her heart she never lost hope. Now it seemed her desire would never be satisfied.

Aquila reentered the room and dragged the cloth from Felice's hand. Felice stepped back as her father's hand came to her elbow, guiding her out of the room.

Duncan Henderson quietly gathered his overseer Mr. Lewis, his bookkeeper Mr. Dunbar, and Mr. Hartly, a white carpenter, after Dr. Bayly confirmed that he could not find what was wrong with Mary Henderson. Bayly gave her more of his mercury pills with the hope that they would somehow cure her of whatever ailed her. Maybe Aquila might have something after all. It would not do any harm to check Mino's hut. These heathen Negroes could be as savage as they wanted to be. He had been told that in some tribes they drank human blood before going into battle and ate the flesh of their captives. He never truly believed that but for some of the things he had seen them do, you could never be sure. Had some of them not been captured and enslaved, God knew what their fates would have been. Perhaps they had even been saved from being eaten by their own kind. They might have done them a good turn removing them from that dark land.

Henderson's relationship with his Negroes over the years was quite different from most of those of his fellow planters. He tried to treat them with fairness but did not hesitate to come down hard on anyone who was insolent or displayed a rebellious attitude. While he had never like Aquila, he felt she might have something there. There would be no harm in it, really. If they found nothing, no one would know he had given in on his doubts about the presence of obeah on his estate.

Felice knew what her father was planning to do. Watching his wife's condition deteriorate had pushed him to consider that maybe Aquila was right. Felice had hoped that he would believe *her* instead that it was possible that the medicine Mary Henderson was taking might be doing her more harm than good. But, Aquila was right. What did a young woman know more than a woman who had seen many storms and lived to tell about them?

That night, Felice snuck from her bed at the sound of voices in the drawing room. The men were gathering to go to Mino's hut. Felice felt her heart leap inside her chest. What will they do to Mino if they did find evidence of obeah working? She admitted there was something about Mino that had made her own blood change to water inside her body the very moment she had met the woman in Mary's hut. Morgie had said she was a warrior woman from the Popo country.

Mino had been one of the women guards to the king as well as being his wife. But she had matched with a Yoruba man, earning herself banishment from the kingdom and a sale to slave traders who had brought her to the colony. Mino had even had her own slaves to do her bidding back in her old country, it was said. Now, she was herself enslaved with no hope of being any other than such. Felice wondered what had happened to her Yoruba man.

The men left the house, their weapons at their waists. Some of them, including her father, had been trained by the militia and often kept watch during times of rebellion or when there were fears of an uprising. Felice felt a tremor run through her body and she decided to follow a distance behind them, hoping she would not be noticed. Their dark path lit by torches, the men proceeded toward the slave quarters. The watchman July jumped quickly onto his feet from his supine position as they approached, exclaiming:

"Mi back! Mi back! Lawd, Massa!"

The men ignored him; perhaps a flogging in the morning for his sleeping on the job would straighten his back out. The quarters were mostly silent except for the intermittent cries of infants who would not or could not sleep. How many would live beyond their first year, born in a dark time and into brutal servitude?

Felice slipped between trees and huts as she followed their steady pace. She sensed eyes in the darkness watching their progress; but, not a breath could be heard. Every now and then, there would be a whistle that seemed to come from high in the trees.

But she knew birds went to their roosts at nightfall. The only one who dared to speak at night was the *Patoo*, its head turning around so its wide eyes could see its prey in the dark of night as it hooted.

The men bent low as they approached the hut Mino occupied alone. Mino was the only woman on the estate who had not been matched with either man or woman. No one had wanted to share a hut with her anyway. She was an amazon of a woman who struck fear in friend and foe alike.

Duncan Henderson's hand rattled against the thin makeshift door of Mino's hut. There was no sound from within. Henderson shook the door again and it fell to the earth, exposing the gaping darkness. The men entered, torches held aloft to lighten the darkness. Felice's eyes opened wide at the sight before her: feathers and bottles hung from the ceiling. Moving closer, Felice gasped at the *yabbas* of bones that were exposed by the torchlight.

"Come out, woman!" Henderson bellowed as he stood in the middle of the hut.

His response was silence, except for the hooting of a *Patoo* in the distance, and Felice knew that Mino was not at home. The woman was long gone. Aquila was right. Mino practiced obeah and there were laws in the colony against that. She could be put to death or transported for having any implements of obeah in her hut.

It was in the year of Felice's birth, the year of Tacky's revolt, that laws had been enacted to restrict the movements of the slaves. No one could walk about without having been given a ticket by the Massa. It was also the year for all free Negroes, Mulattos, and Indians to be registered and given certificates of registration, their badge of freedom, to prove that they were indeed not one of the enslaved.

Some believed that the slaves of the rebellion had used certain powers to render themselves invisible to the eyes of the whites, resulting in severe trouncing of the enemy in their battles with the militia. Had it not been for the Maroons and dissention among the ranks, the enslaved would have certainly been victorious.

Somehow, Felice wished they had caught Mino. By now, she must have joined the Maroons in some cave and would never be found. She just hoped the woman would never show herself on the estate again. If she had really been able to make Mary Henderson ill, then there was no telling what else she could do. Somewhere, deep inside of her, Felice still believed that Mary Henderson's illness was not as a result of Mino's or anyone else's machinations.

In the light of morning, Duncan Henderson ordered that Mino's hut be torn down and its contents destroyed. Suddenly, all able bodied men were ailing and needed to be sent to the Negro House to be treated. Henderson suspected they were all afraid of coming into contact with the parrot's teeth and dog's teeth and grave dirt they had found in the hut. Henderson flogged Adam and Billy who had no verifiable complaint and ordered them to get to work pulling down the small wattle and daub structure.

As the men pulled at the hut, there was a sudden rush as if something had freed itself from the walls. They ran, swearing like sailors while calling out to their gods to save them. They could not be found on the estate for the balance of the day.

The demolition of Mino's hut was completed by the carpenter Mr. Hartly, another white carpenter Mr. Clark who had lately come to the estate, and two of their Negro boys who had been hired out from Mr. Ramsey's plantation for the day. Henderson promised he would deal with each of his renegades in turn with appropriate punishment and time in the bilboes. That will teach them to be insolent and disobedient. He gave Tony and Asherry tickets to go in search of Mino. Adam and Billy had not returned. They were now runaways along with Tony and Asherry who, after three days, did not return to Greenrock. Henderson placed an advertisement in the *Cornwall Chronicle* with a reward of a *pistole* each for the return of his five slaves, including Mino. He did not care for Mino's return; he would only have to transport her to America or Cuba. Somewhere inside him was a small fear of what he did not know about.

Mary Henderson was becoming weaker each day and still Dr. Bayly could not find an answer for her ailment. He came, he bled her, and she got weaker.

"May I suggest, Mr. Henderson, that you take her to Bluefields Bay," Felice said one morning at breakfast.

She had read enough on how a change of air could do a body good. Her father looked up. Rebecca and young Duncan sat straight-backed, cutting at their food. They were now as dark as it was possible for them to get without looking like Mulattos or Negroes. The good thing for them was that they only had to shield themselves from the harsh tropical sun for a few days to return to their pure state. They would never be mistaken for the enslaved.

Rebecca was growing tall and her dresses were becoming too short for her rather quickly. She often wore her hair in two ribboned plaits which hung to the sides of her head, giving her an impish appearance. Her brother was closely following her and promised to soon be taller than his sister. They would soon be off to meet with their morose tutor Brooks, and remain with him for most of the morning. It was perhaps time for Rebecca to learn how to embroider and do the other things required of a young woman; but her mother was in no condition to make any decisions for herself or for her children.

They had hardly seen their mother of late; they just knew that she was unwell. Felice felt sorry for them not knowing how precariously their mother was clinging to life.

"Whatever do you mean, Felice?" her father asked as he forked a piece of boiled yam into his mouth.

The scent of cooked liver was strong in the room. Cook had outdone herself again if it was possible for her to do that. Whatever she put in her pot was a secret she would take to her grave. Duncan Henderson could not imagine eating and enjoying anyone else's cooking.

"I have read that the sea air is good for restoring the spirit," she explained.

He looked at her as if in deep thought.

"You might have something there, I daresay. I am also

thinking we should stop the mercury pills. I don't believe they are helping her anymore."

"What is wrong with Mother?" Rebecca inquired, looking from one to the other.

It was strange how they now seemed to be a family. Felice could not tell when they had begun having conversations over a meal or when her father had started involving her in decisions. Even the children seemed to treat her as an equal now, often regaling her with tales of their day's exploits. Maybe it was since Mary Henderson's illness. Or maybe it was since her betrothal to John McDowell.

John. Felice's heart fluttered somewhere in her chest. He had left for business with his father to Falmouth, Spanish Town, and Kingston almost a fortnight before and it seemed like forever before he returned. He promised to escort her to the theatre in Montego Bay on his return. *A Dish of Mr. Foot's Tea* was set to be performed in Montego Bay by the American Company of Comedians and his father had secured tickets for them.

"Your mother is doing fine, Becca," Henderson explained, "just a bit under the weather."

"I see. Well, I hope she gets better soon," Rebecca answered.

"May we then accompany her to Bluefields Bay, Father?"

"We will see about that. I believe your sister has a splendid idea here."

Felice paused with the fork halfway to her mouth. Sister? Had her father just referred to her as sister to Rebecca? She looked up at him and their eyes locked. He nodded back at her and she gave him a small smile.

And so Mary Henderson was shuttled off to Bluefields Bay with the plan that she would remain for the next three months with a Mrs. Beckford, Mr. Beckford a merchant, and their daughters the Misses Beckford, and where she could see the ocean and listen to the lapping of the waves calling her home. Maybe someday they would bring her back to her home. For now, she could dream while she recovered from whatever calamity this godforsaken place had brought upon her.

The shadowy, creeping figure startled Felice as she hurried down the steps of Greenrock Estate. Her eyes locked with those of the woman who had the ability to make her blood run cold within her veins. Mino. Felice opened her mouth but not a sound came out.

It had been two months since the woman had disappeared.

The men had returned to the estate, been flogged for their unauthorized absences despite their excuses of searching for Mino and following the trails others had sent them on, and had since returned to their labors. Mino had chosen to remain free. What was she doing on the estate?

Mino hurried off into the darkness and Felice stood for a moment, wondering if there was something afoot. Mino probably came to steal food. Maybe she lived in the bushes and came at night to gather what she could in order to stay alive. With her house torn down, she probably had nowhere to lay her head. Everyone was afraid of her, except perhaps for Quaco and Mary, so no one would want to shelter her.

There were always complaints of missing provisions. Each slave family or grouping had a small piece of land to plant provisions and too often they would report that someone had raided their ground in the night. There were goats stolen and chickens slaughtered in the dark of night. July, the watchman, was too often flogged for falling asleep and not knowing what had happened. He never changed the habits that perhaps kept him alive when he knew a renegade or two was on the property in search of sustenance. It was better to risk a flogging from the Massa than to be slaughtered or maimed by a renegade because he reported what he had seen in the cover of night.

Felice hurried off to where John waited under the tamarind tree, dismissing Mino from her thoughts. His figure detached itself from the tree and she rushed to his arms. His lips came down on hers and Felice felt a breathless rush. She felt the tingling to the tips of her breasts and warmth rushed through her body. He released her and she clung to him for a moment.

Wordlessly, he helped her up onto Brutus before joining her.

They rode in silence, Felice inhaling the scent of him and reveling in the feel of his chest against her back as he held her close.

"How do you feel, Felice?" he whispered against her hair.

"I feel good, John," she whispered back.

"Like a Missis?"

"Yes."

"Like you could rule the entire world?"

"Yes."

"Like this is all yours and everyone does your bidding without question?"

"Yes, John. I am Missis of this estate. They will obey me."

She knew he was smiling. It was a game they played each time they met like this. They were powerful in the dark of the night where no one could see the shade of skin that made all the difference. They rode along the river for a while and then John turned Brutus in a new direction. Felice glanced up at him in the darkness but he did not explain.

They left the estate onto the track that led off the estate and Felice felt her heart leap.

"Where are we going?" she whispered.

He smiled down at her but she did not see it. For a while they rode in silence until he turned the horse off the road and onto a bushy path. Then he stopped and slid off the horse before helping her down. He tethered Brutus to a tree and held her hand, guiding her forward.

"Where are we?"

"Don't worry."

Felice felt a small excitement flutter in her chest; she wasn't sure why. She was somewhat afraid but somehow felt secure with John. As he led her forward, a small tremor passed through her that had nothing to do with the chill of the night. Suddenly, they became aware of sounds and small movements ahead. John pulled her down to the ground and motioned her to be quiet as they squatted. He separated the bushes that were obscuring their view.

In the clearing was a small abandoned hut in which a group was gathered around a low, flickering flame. Felice gasped softly as she recognized Mino in the center of the group of perhaps a dozen. John grabbed Felice's hand and motioned to her that they needed to leave. Felice's heart thudded inside her chest. Slowly, they backed away until they reached where Brutus stood quietly as if he too knew the need for silence.

John led his horse away, Felice's hand secure in his. When they reached the road, he mounted and pulled her up in front of him. Slowly they rode off until he was sure their sounds could not be detected. Then he kicked at Brutus's sides, sending the horse into a gallop.

Felice could feel his tight grip against her chest while his other hand grasped the reins. Brutus' hooves pounded in the dark night as they headed for McDowell's estate at breakneck speed. The breeze whipped against her face and through her hair. She closed her eyes tightly against the sting of the breeze.

Sliding down from the horse even before it stopped, John dashed for the house when they arrived, leaving Felice to follow.

"Father! Father!" he hollered as he rushed in through the side door and into the hallway, Felice behind him.

They could hear stirrings throughout the house and candles were being lit. McDowell shuffled from his room, a candle illuminating his features as he stood on the landing peering into the darkness of the hallway.

"What goes on down there?" McDowell thundered as he shone the light into the darkness.

"Father! They are plotting," John shouted breathlessly.

"Who? What?"

"The slaves. They are meeting in the old hut on Leith's near the *barcadier*," John explained as he tried to calm himself.

His father stared down at him. Behind him John's mother stood in the shadows; her eyes were focused on the shadowy figure behind her son. It did not need much for her to know who was standing behind her John.

Soon the whole household was astir, including John's Aunt

Ethel who was visiting her brother. Felice slipped into the shadows, hoping no one had noticed her presence. Yes, she was betrothed to John; but at this late hour, it was not seemly for any young unmarried woman, even a mulatto one, to be seen alone in the company of a man who was not her father or brother.

Riders were dispatched forthwith to Greenrock and other estates and plantations around. They could only arm themselves as it was unsure whether the slaves were planning a strike that very night. There had been nothing in the past few days to indicate that anything was amiss. Often you could almost smell it in the air. They became more barefaced and insolent. They became more resistant as if preparing their minds and bodies for battle. When they would strike was a matter left to the one good Negro who would inform his master about the plans of his fellows, or the intervention of Providence. Many an insurrection had been prevented or quelled when a slave or two felt it unjust that his brothers and sisters in bondage decided to revolt against the ones who fed and clothed them at no charge; all they asked for was servitude in return. Why would they want to bite the hands that fed them?

"John," Felice called in a soft whisper from her position behind the drapes in the drawing room.

He seemed to have forgotten about her in the flurry of activities that had followed his arrival. He seemed startled to see her there.

"I must get back to Greenrock. I am not supposed to be here."

He seemed puzzled for a moment.

"It might not be safe to leave now, Felice."

"But, I must get back. They will realize that I am not home. There will be a panic. Even now, it might be too late."

"I will speak to my father."

It was a long few minutes before John returned with news that his father would have her escorted home in a carriage with James, a driver. John insisted on accompanying her. Felice could well imagine how her father, and Cook would feel if they found her missing.

The carriage seemed to progress slowly until they finally saw the lights of Greenrock. There were people moving around in the darkness and Felice slipped in among them, praying she did not meet with her mother or father. She hurried to her room but met Cook coming down the stairs.

"Felice, where you been?"

"What do you mean?"

"I mean where you coming from?"

"None of your business."

"Lissen to me, Felice, I no fraid fi slap you right yasso. Why you not in yuh room?"

"May I remind you that I am the master's daughter? I don't

have to answer to you."

Cook stared at her daughter. Her face was contorted in shock and anger.

"I went riding with John if you must know," Felice finally explained.

"Riding? At dis time a night? Felice, if Mass John doan married you, you only fit to be a whore. Not even Missa Evan want you den. Felice, be careful. Doan lay yourself careless, even fi Mass John."

Felice stood silent, her eyes downcast in shame. How could she have spoken to her own mother in that way? Granted she was a slave; but she was still her mother. Cook had watched over her all her life the way a hen watched over her chickens. She would get into a flurry if she thought her child was about to be hurt. She only wanted to see good for her daughter. All her life, Felice had never really given a thought as to why the cook of the estate took so much interest in her well-being. It always just seemed like the master had simply put the woman in charge of the mulatto girl he had sired with one of his slaves.

Suddenly, Cook pulled the girl to her bosom and held her the way she used to through a stormy night. As quickly, she released Felice and continued down the stairs toward her own room. Felice stood, ashamed of her behavior. She hurried to her room and threw herself on the bed. It was going to be a long night for everyone.

The militia was on high alert for the next fortnight and movement between plantations was restricted. Felice did not see John in that time but received messages and gifts from him by way of slaves who were trusted enough to carry on the business of their masters. Then there was calm and everyone believed it had been a false alarm.

Mino's illuminated face kept flashing before Felice's eyes. Shivers ran through her body at the memory of the expression on the woman's face. It was entirely possible that the woman was only practicing her obeah; Felice did not know what that looked like. It had been in secret and in the dark of night; who knew what spirits the woman was calling up. But somehow, Felice was not convinced. There was just something about the way the bodies were huddled and how the men stood around as if they were getting their bodies ready for battle.

Everything soon moved back to normal and the planters were happy again that they had once more foiled an attempt by the ingrates to murder them in their beds.

Cook's admonition replayed in Felice's mind again and again. She now knew what John had planned that night. What other reason did he have for taking her to the old hut? Somewhere inside the thought made her feel unclean. Why would he take his betrothed to an old slave hut in the dark of night? And she had willingly gone along. She sent him a note that it might not be wise to meet again at night until they were married. He returned a note apologizing for his behavior; but Providence had been on their side since they might have thwarted a revolt that night, he said.

The Master's Daughter   Vjange Hazle

CHAPTER 9

"We are neglected, I tell you," Duncan Henderson exclaimed over his drink. "They need to end that dratted war, man."

"You are right, Henderson. We have absolutely no protection from the damned rebels," McDowell added.

The group of five was sitting in the drawing room, weapons at their sides. They were taking no chances, even though threats of rebellion had passed and everyone seemed happy in their servitude. They had not had to do any unusual whippings among the slaves. Even William Bernard of Flamstead had not used the *manati* skin or sea cow hide of late on his slaves.

"Everything is focused on America. We have little to no defense. We are ripe, I tell you," Mr. Bernard suggested.

It had only been a few months before that the colonists had applauded the governor and the king for their success in routing the rebels in North America. It was this focus of the military on North America that was making the planters uneasy. They were grossly underprepared to defend themselves if the slaves decided that this was the time for rebellion. It would not be the first time the bastards took advantage of this opportunity. The new laws to prevent a repeat of those occurrences were evidence of that.

The Maroons were fulfilling the obligation of their treaty

signed near forty years before. Only last Sunday the Trelawny Town Maroons had found some runaways, killed three of them, and were off to rout another band of runaways. The government had fortified barracks and more planters were being trained and armed by the militia. But it was still not enough. The feeling of unease was all across the colony. It did not help that there were now even those in the colony speaking against slavery, inciting the Negroes to disobey their masters; that no one should be enslaved, no matter their race. There were those preaching equality of free and enslaved as they pointed to the Scriptures. Of all the absurdities!

John sat uneasily next to his father. Although he should be concerned with the conversation around him, his mind was on Felice. Dinner had been somewhat awkward. It was the first time they were seeing each other since the night they had discovered the possible plot. Felice had avoided his eyes. She was sitting next to her father pretending interest in the conversation. John tried to catch her eye but she was not looking his way.

Despite his apology, Felice still could not believe he had thought so little of her. Cook was right; what if he did not marry her? Then she would have no choice but to be mistress to Mr. Evan. How could John place her in that position? She glanced up and he was standing next to her.

"May I speak with you a moment, Felice," he asked in a low whisper.

Her father glanced at her and nodded. Rising, she placed her hand in the crook of John's arm and they walked together to the verandah. Felice looked up at the inky darkness of the night sky. The stars seemed more numerous than she had ever seen them. Suddenly, a light dashed across the sky and she felt a small shiver as she gazed at the beauty of the lights that quickly disappeared.

"My dear, Felice," he began. "I cannot say enough how sorry I am. It was foolish of me to treat you so common. I just wanted to be with you. To hold you close to me. When I kiss you, you cannot understand what that does to me."

Felice was silent as she stood with her back to him. He stood a decent distance from her, his hands folded into each other in front of him.

"We can't be married soon enough. I want you for my wife, Felice. I want to ask Father for us to move our wedding forward, if that is alright with you."

"Yes, John," she finally responded, turning to face him. "I feel the same about you too. I think about you and being close to you all the time. If only we could be married tomorrow."

John gave a small laugh.

"I don't believe we can get a special license that quickly."

"You know what I mean."

"I promise to never do that to you again."

"Thank you, John."

"So, are you ready for the horse races in the morning?"

"Yes, everyone will be going. My father has given everyone the day off."

"How generous of him," John commented, a note of amusement in his tone. "I have missed you, though."

"It can't be helped. I think we should be careful, John. After all, we can't go coupling like the slaves do, can we?"

There were movements inside and they realized that the men were rising to take their leave. Quickly, John planted a kiss on her lips, grinning at her as he extended his arm. Felice slapped him playfully as the taste of him lingered on her lips. Inside her heart was a bubbling feeling. She was happy to hear him say he wanted to marry her quickly.

The party departed and Felice returned to the verandah to relive the moments she had just spent with John. The place settled into a calm but still she stood watching the night. Not even the frogs were croaking tonight; neither were the crickets singing their loud song.

"Ahem."

Duncan Henderson cleared his throat behind her. Felice turned to face him.

"Are you alright, Felice?" he asked, hands behind his back.

"Yes, sir. It is such a beautiful night."

"Indeed it is. Indeed it is. That is one of the reasons I love the colony. The beauty of the nights."

"You love the colony, sir?"

"I must admit I do."

"You don't like Scotland, then?"

"Oh, I love my homeland."

"Do you ever miss it?"

"At times, yes. At times. But here, I am master of my own destiny. Except for those confounded rebels, I can walk about as I please."

"Will you ever go back there to live then, sir?"

"I don't know, my dear. It is a hard life in the colony. I have never worked this hard in all my life. But I am satisfied at the end of the day that all of this is mine," he said, spreading his hands to encompass all that he owned, man and beast.

Felice was silent. She wanted to ask him if he would ever free her mother and sister. Perhaps she already knew the answer so it was better left unasked. What if he freed all his slaves and paid them wages? It would not be much different from what he now did in hiring them out now and then and giving them tickets to go and sell goods for him. He paid them from the results of their commerce. All he needed to do was sign their free papers and let them go. She was sure they would remain on the estate as his workers.

"Is everything alright with John?" he continued.

"Yes, sir. It is. He wants to move our wedding forward. I agree with him."

"Are you sure now?"

"I think it is the wise thing to do."

Duncan Henderson was silent as he tried to read her expression in the half-light.

"Alright then. If that is what you want. I will speak to McDowell. Felice, I am sorry I ever thought to give you over to Evan. I was only thinking of your future. You are much too beautiful, much too keen, to be just mistress to an old decrepit like Evan."

A small giggle escaped her lips. Her father described his friend well.

"Well, my dear, don't remain too long in the moonlight. It is late and it is not safe."

"I will turn in in a moment, sir. Goodnight then. I will have Quaco lock up."

Henderson nodded and turned inside. Felice knew it was not safe to remain in the darkness but it felt so good to have the night air on her face and to listen to the silence. There were not that many still nights; there were always the night creatures calling out from their crevices. A sudden movement caught Felice's eye.

They moved soundlessly as if their feet were one with the earth, the dark their disguise and guide. Felice shuffled to hide behind a post on the verandah. The small group of scantily clad men and women walked by, their faces focused forward. A woman turned her head, her eyes seeming to penetrate the dark. Mino. Felice was sure the woman had seen her as she stood for long moments as if willing Felice to show herself. Mino's red eyes seemed to glow in the dark and Felice felt a small shiver go through her body. The group moved on and Felice stood still, sure Mino had remained behind.

It seemed a long while before Felice felt she could breathe again. Stooping to be level with the rails of the verandah, she shuffled her way back into the house, bumping into Quaco who seemed to have been coming to find her. Her eyes moved from his bare feet, up his trousered leg, and up to his face. He smiled down at her.

"Miss Felice," he greeted, "what you doing, ma'am?"

"Nothing, Quaco," she responded as she stood to face him. "I just wondered what it would be like to be a short person. You may lock up now."

"Yes, miss. You have a good sleep now."

"You too, Quaco. Goodnight."

Her heart pounding, Felice wondered if Quaco knew what was about to happen or if he was a part of it. She tried not to hurry up the stairs and to her father's suite of rooms, just in case Quaco was watching. Her soft knock sounded on her father's door. She just hoped he had not yet fallen asleep. She knocked again, a bit more firmly this time. It felt like long moments before she heard him shuffling toward the door and then it opened. Henderson's face had a puzzled look as he wrapped his robe around his body. Felice had the feeling he wore nothing under it.

"I think there is something afoot, sir. I just saw Mino and a group..."

Henderson did not wait for her to finish as he dashed for his weapon.

"Go down to Isabella," he commanded.

"What?"

"Your mother. Go!"

Felice's hesitation was only momentary. She hurried behind him as he dashed down the stairs. Knocking softly on Cook's door, Felice waited anxiously for her mother to open to her. Cook's face appeared in the darkness through a crack in the door. She opened wider to her daughter.

"What happen, Felice?" the woman inquired as she wrapped her nightdress more tightly around her body.

"Something happening. Where Morgie?"

Morgie woke from her sleep and sat up in the bed.

"Wha she doing here?" Morgie barked at sight of her sister.

"Shhh!" their mother commanded. "What going on, Felice?" Cook continued, a note of anxiety in her voice.

Glad to see that her sister was not part of what was about to happen, Felice explained. Cook reached under her bed and pulled out a bill and a pistol. Felice's eyes opened wide. Morgie pulled out her own weapons from their similar hiding place. The girl's eyes gleamed in the darkness.

"Mino shoulda neva did come back," Morgie said. "She shoulda did stay where she gone."

Felice felt a shiver go through her body as she took in the gleam of the sharp edges of the large knives that were meant to cut cane. She wondered if either woman had ever used their weapons.

Shuffling sounds from outside reached their hearing. Felice sat on her mother's bed, wishing she too was armed; wishing she had learned to swing the bill. She felt helpless as the night became alive with sounds. She recalled the earlier silence. It was as if the night creatures themselves had known that the night would erupt in mayhem.

Shouts came from outside and Cook opened her door to peer out. There was no one about in the Great House but they could hear voices and the beating of drums. The sound of pistols being fired echoed into the night amid shouts and screams. Suddenly, there was the smell of smoke and Felice's eyes opened wide.

Cook hurried her daughters out of the room, realizing that someone had set the house afire. As they hurried out, a figure blocked their path. Mino stood, a bill in each hand, their blades glistening.

"Pass me di malatta," Mino ground out.

"Yuh haffi come through me, you know, Mino," Cook challenged.

"Move outa di way," the warrior woman commanded.

"Mek me."

The women eyed each other in the dimly lit room as Felice stood behind her mother. The smell of smoke was strong in their nostrils and they could hear shouts as men and women rushed toward the house with pails of water, hoping to save it from destruction. Absently, Felice wondered about Rebecca and Young Duncan. Their father would have kept them safe. He had sent *her* to safety; how much more would he care for the children of his marriage; the ones born of the mother country. Although now, Felice was not sure how safe she was as she stared into the reddened eyes of the woman who hated her so.

Cook stood facing Mino, Morgie at her side. Cook's pistol was in her left hand, her bill in her right. Morgie's right arm rose and she pointed her pistol at Mino, her left hand, from which her bill glistened, supporting the right.

The room erupted in sound and soon they were surrounded by armed men and women. Mino stood her ground, her body poised for action as she glanced around, her arms outstretched, pointing the blades in a dare toward the group. Mino turned around in a circle, her eyes darting from face to face. She knew she was surrounded but Felice was sure the woman would not go down without a fight.

A loud report stilled the room and Felice watched as Mino's eyes widened. The woman glanced down at her dress and the bills fell from her hands. It seemed like a moment frozen. Blood seeped from the woman's bosom. Her fall, in a heap, was soundless.

Duncan Henderson marched into the room and, with his foot, pressed at the body of the fallen woman. His weapon was clutched in his hand. The smoke was pressing in on them and Henderson ordered them out.

"Becca and Duncan?" Felice asked quickly in between her coughs.

"They are safe. Now, hurry out."

They hurried out the front door amid the shouts of those who were desperately trying to save the Great House. Duncan Henderson bent to retrieve Mino's body. If she was not dead, she would hang for this. He walked out into the night, Mino's body thrown like a bag of potatoes over his shoulder.

Greenrock Estate was not completely burned to the ground.

The slaves had saved much of the place that was the source of their life. Where would they have gone had the estate been destroyed? They had to save it at all costs. Some had wanted to be part of the rebellion. They had been told; but only few had decided to take part. Some of them knew it just was not the right time. On top of that, it was being led by Mino, the warrior woman. Her desire was not for freedom but for revenge. She had wanted to be the one to execute the Massa's mulatto daughter; the girl who was a constant reminder of her own state of helplessness in servitude.

Most of them had watched little Felice grow to become a woman. She was Cook's daughter, for God's sake, sister to Morgiana who herself worked the fields alongside them. As a child, she had played with their children until the Massa decided she did not belong with them. The girl had done no one wrong. Her only sin was to be born the master's daughter and a mulatto. Mino's cause was not their cause. Only Adam, Billy, Asherry, and Tony had agreed to be a part of it. They had received their deserts.

There were thirty executions, particularly in Hanover and Westmoreland. Ringleaders and their accomplices were quickly discovered before the rebellion even began. The Navy and Militia had been on hand, to the dismay of the rebels. The plantation owners had been on high alert for a while; all were armed for such an incident. Mino was but a small part of this insurrection and she was brought low by a shot from her master's pistol. Her body was hung high like the others as a reminder of the penalties for rebelling; some were quartered; others burned. The John Crows, perhaps aware they were protected by a law that provided no protection for the Negroes, gathered for their feast, their entitlement, as they circled on high. The rebellion was quelled even as the rebels thought about it; this was the lesson to be learned for all other ingrates in the future who thought to rebel against their masters.

"Outrageous!" bellowed William Bernard. "How can they justly complain about their lives?"

"Their lives are as easy as any overseer's," George Beckford added.

"Their food is plentiful, if I may say so," Evan growled. "They practically feed themselves from their own grounds that *we* give them. I give them the hog and cow tripe at no cost to them. I cannot fathom why they would want to kill us. They probably eat better than we do, if I might add."

The night of bloodshed still played in Felice's mind, both in her waking and sleeping moments and the scent of smoke and fire lingered in the furniture and in the window drapes all around the Great House. She begged Morgie to come and stay with her at night since she woke up in sweats, Mino's face swimming before her eyes even as she struggled to escape her nightmares.

Felice smiled to herself as she recalled the first night Morgie came to stay with her. A bath was drawn in the large wooden tub Felice used when the occasion called for it. Morgie shivered slightly as she climbed in and sank down into the cool water. It was so different from bathing in the river where there was always the danger of crocodiles. Quaco's Mary poured water from a pitcher on top of the girl's wooly head. She soaped Morgie's head and washed her hair. Felice grinned at her sister as the girl affected 'Missis' behavior.

Her hair rubbed dry, Morgie paraded herself, trying on her sister's clothing and pretending she was no longer a slave but mistress of her own destiny. Her hair free from being tied down, she grabbed her sister's brush; but it was too soft for her locks. She contented herself with twisting her hair into *Bantu* knots, exploring the pomades on the bureau and trying on the gold and pearl hair brooch and other hair combs. Then, her play complete, she sank into bed in one of Felice's nightgowns.

"You so far," Morgiana called to her sister from one edge of the bed.

Felice smiled. It was good to have her sister Morgie back again.

So Morgie slept next to Felice in her soft bed. And Felice felt safe, knowing that next to her lay a warrior woman who knew how to fight.

Mary Henderson's quarters were severely damaged and the children's suite smelled too strongly of smoke to be habitable. Fortunately, the woman had remained with the Beckford's another two months. It would be some time before she returned to Greenrock.

Felice looked across at John where he sat at the table next to his father. The McDowell's estate had been saved. None of their slaves had joined the rebellion; but, had Felice not raised the alarm, it would only have been a matter of time before Mino and her followers, joined by others, would have got to them. The massacre would have been written about for centuries to come. A revolt foiled will become lost in history; its mention only a line, not enough for even a page in a history book.

Their marriage was to be in two months. Felice was already fitted for her dress and John was measured for his suit. A feeling of excitement filled her each time she thought about being joined with John. She hoped nothing would come up to change their plans again. They had kept themselves circumspect, Cook's admonition always ringing in her ears.

The Master's Daughter   Vjange Hazle

CHAPTER 10

Quaco sat staring at Mary, his Afua, where she lay on the small bed they shared. A tear formed in the corner of one eye. His Mary was laid up and he did not know what to do. Although he never really liked the woman Mino, he had to admit she had done much in the dark of night to save the life of many a slave. What concoctions she used, no one knew; they only knew that they could walk from their beds when she was done with them and back to the miserable slavery that was their life.

Sometimes he thought maybe it would be best to not be made well but to go the way of the ancestors. The land of his ancestors was now a distant memory; the faces of his people had become one in the tumult of the colony. Quaco knew the only way to return to his land was to fly away on the wings of freedom; but he could not leave his Afua behind to suffer. If only he had the wings of a dove he would take them both back to the land from which they had been torn. He would fly away and find rest.

The night of Mino's revolt was still clear in his mind. What if he had not been there to protect his Mary? Duncan Henderson had placed him in charge of his two children Rebecca and Duncan and he had shuttled them off to his hut where Mary waited. The children had sat, cowering in fear at the unfamiliar surroundings of a slave hut. There was no comfortable place for them to rest. The place was not built to accommodate the children of a Massa. Mary had armed herself like so long ago when she had fought like a warrior to help trounce the militia. But she no longer had the strength she once did. She could no longer hold the weapon strong in her hand and her fire burned, though with diminished force.

A fever burned Mary's forehead and Quaco wet it with a rag like he had seen Mino do. What she put in the water was her mystery and her knowledge had gone with her. Samson entered the hut.

The boy had become such a man. It was time for him to match with a woman on the estate but he was taking his time. Quaco had suggested they build a hut for him but Samson said "in time". He was already matched with Cook's Morgiana, anyway. What was he waiting for? He was seventeen. It was time.

"How she do?" Samson asked as he threw a sack down on the dirt floor.

"She hot, man. We might haffi ask Massa fi get Dr. Bayly."

"I go get Morgie. She wi know wha fi do."

"You tink so?"

"She learn a lickle from Mino but she no waan nobody know."

"Awright den. Hurry so come back."

Samson exited the hut and hurried through the night back to

the Great House. Tall John, who was serving as butler for the evening opened the door to him. Heading to Cook's room he rapped on the door.

"Morgie wid Felice," Cook responded to his query when she opened to him. "Me go call har fi yuh."

Cook headed up the stairs and returned with both daughters in tow. Samson explained the need. Morgie hurried to her room and pulled a bag from under her bed. Felice glanced at the bag with a look of suspicion. What could Morgie have in that bag? Was she working obeah? Morgie ignored her and led the way out the door. Samson followed. Felice hesitated and then decided she had to see what her sister did. Could she have a sister who was an obeah woman?

Morgiana ignored Felice as the group made its way through the darkness along the well-worn path between the Great House and the slave quarters. A small light burned in the hut as they entered. Morgie hurried to Mary's side. Felice glanced at Quaco who sat helpless on the dirt floor, a rag in his hand. His eyes lighted hopefully as Morgie bent over his Afua.

Felice watched as Morgie pulled a calabash bowl from her bag. The girl then placed leaves and bushes in the bowl and began to crush them together. A strange smell filled the air and for a moment Felice was frightened. Was this what they called obeah? It did not seem that way to Felice. Could Mino have been a medicine woman and not an obeah woman? What if they thought Morgie was an obeah woman too? A small fear ran through Felice.

Wrapping the pounded substance in a cloth, Morgie placed it on Mary's forehead declaring, "it wi draw di fever." She proceeded to light a piece of bush and turned the four corners of the hut as she waved the smoke around, mumbling inaudibly. Felice's eyes opened wide. She wondered if their mother knew what Morgie did.

The ritual completed, Morgie promised to return early in the morning when the fever should break. Samson walked with them back to the Great House. The group was silent. Felice still could not believe what she had just seen. At the door of the Great House, Samson lingered.

"Gwaan inside, Miss Felice. Me soon come," Morgie whispered.

As Felice entered the house, she turned to see Samson and Morgie embrace. As slaves, they could not marry unless they were free. They would, quite likely, live together as a match; but they could not do what she and John were about to do in a short while. Marrying was not for the enslaved. They could couple and produce offspring; but they could never become husband and wife according to the law.

It was much later that Morgie snuck into the room and slipped silently into the bed. Felice pretended to be asleep, but somehow she knew she had not convinced Morgie. Her sister, though younger, was much wiser.

It was almost time for her marriage to John McDowell and Felice found it hard to contain herself. They scarcely spent time together alone and were often accompanied to the theatre in Montego Bay by both their fathers. John's mother never attended and Mary Henderson was now due to return before the wedding. She missed being able to ride with John at night but now knew it was not safe in more ways than one. It would not do for either of them to come to harm before they were joined in matrimony.

The ceremony itself was to be performed at the McDowell Estate where the bride and groom would reside. Felice still could not believe that it was almost here.

Her nightmares slowly ceased and Morgie returned to the room she shared with her mother. Felice felt so alone now that she was the only one sleeping in the big bed, which at one time had seemed to swallow her up. That would soon change and she would be sharing a bed with her husband. A thrill ran through her.

She wrapped her arms around her body as she gazed up at the night sky. It had somehow become her habit to stand on the verandah and watch the lights peeping through the inky darkness. She often wondered what was there beyond the stars. Felice wished she had paid more attention to her readings on astronomy. It all had seemed too much like they were guessing and giving names to objects just because they could. She had preferred getting absorbed in medical books that discussed the ailments of the body; and tales like those of Constantia Phillips, the counterfeit Lady whose scandalous life had rocked Europe, had titillated her senses. Soon, she too would understand what sweetness the lady had written about. Absently, Felice wondered what had become of Miss Rutherfurd. If only she knew that little Felice was about to be married and become a woman.

Felice turned at the sound behind her, expecting to see Quaco. His Mary had recovered under the ministrations of young Morgie. Felice now saw her sister in a new light. Whether she was really an obeah woman or not, Morgie had the ability to heal, that much Felice knew.

Felice frowned when a dark stranger appeared from one corner of the verandah. Before she could react, another dark stranger appeared next to her and Felice felt her heart leap. A hand clasped itself across her mouth and another grabbed her around the waist at the same time. The smell of earth filled her nostrils as the rough, dirty hand pressed itself against her mouth. Someone grabbed her feet and both men lifted her off the floor. Felice began to struggle against her captors but their grip on her was firm. The men leaped over the railing of the verandah as they threw her to waiting hands below. She felt as if the wind was knocked out of her as she landed on human flesh. Her mouth was quickly covered and a piece of rough cloth tied around her eyes. Everything became pitch dark.

Felice kicked out, grunting and squealing as best she could; but it was to no avail. The men, it seemed four in all, had her tightly in their grip as they bound her hands and feet and tied a dirty tasting rag across her mouth. She was thrown across the back of an animal, perhaps a mule and the men led the animal off. No one uttered a word as they led the animal away from Greenrock and into the night.

As the group left the estate behind, they picked up some speed with one man jumping on the back of the mule and riding with Felice before him, a hand on her back to secure her. She could hear the others running. They had not exchanged a word all this time.

Felice's body ached as she bounced across the mule's back, her head hanging down. She felt she must surely pass out as she felt the blood going to her head and she tried to raise her head to keep it from getting too heavy. It seemed they had been riding for a long time when they finally stopped. There was no way to know where they were and there was an eerie silence about the place. She felt her heart beating in her chest.

Felice sensed that someone else had arrived as she was lifted off the back of the animal and made to stand on her feet. She rocked unsteadily as she tried to gain her balance and a rough hand reached out to steady her. No one said a word.

There was a stillness and then she heard a shuffling around. She felt herself being lifted again and being carried up steps. Where was she? Then she was again made to stand, this time on what felt like a wooden floor. The bindings were removed from her mouth and feet but her hands were still held securely and her eyes covered. Another silence followed and she realized then that she was now alone with the new stranger. She could sense a scrutiny and Felice felt a moment of panic.

A hand touched her waist, then began a journey across her

body, coming to rest on a breast. Felice shrunk from the unaccustomed touch. She knew this was not John. The touch was unfamiliar; but she felt it was a man's hand.

"What do you want?" Felice demanded, trying to quell the fear that was rising to her throat.

There was no response. The hand continued its exploration to her other breast.

"Who are you?"

A soft, masculine chuckle was her response. Suddenly, she heard a ripping sound and realized that the front of her dress had been torn open. She felt her body shiver as the cold air touched her skin. No, this must not be! The hands paused in their roving and Felice could hear movements around the room. Then the footsteps came near and she could smell the tobacco and rum on the man's breath. *No! No!* her mind screamed.

"Please, sir. Have some respect for my father," Felice said in a half pleading tone.

A rough hand came up to touch one of her breasts and Felice felt a shiver run through her body as an arm circled her waist. Then a warm wetness surrounded one nipple and she realized his mouth was on her skin. Felice pushed at him with her bound hands and let out a piercing scream while she struggled against him. A stinging slap across her face was the response and she fell to the floor.

The cloth binding her eyes was ripped from her face and she looked up into the red eyes of Mr. Evan as he bent over her.

"Please don't do this, Mr. Evan," she pleaded.

Felice found herself in a bedroom. It was a small one with little furniture and did not seem to be used often or made for comfort. In the center was a roughly hewn bed such as a man might have in a cottage in the bushes when he cannot make it home for the night. Felice's face hurt from the slap and she could feel the tears coming.

Dragging her to sit upright, he stooped to face her.

"Thought you were too good for me, didn't you?" Evan growled, his face close to Felice's. "Now, we'll see who is too good for whom."

Roughly, he pulled her up to a standing position and proceeded to rip the balance of her dress from her body, leaving her only in her drawers and the slippers on her feet. Felice felt the tears spring to her eyes.

"Please, Mr. Evan."

"Shut your mouth and take what's coming to you!"

He lifted her and dumped her onto the bed. But he did not join her. Instead, he went to a small table by the door and it was then that Felice noticed the whip laying there among a clutter of other things like knives, mugs and plates.

"No, sir! No, sir," she pleaded. "Please, Mr. Evan."

Slowly, he turned around, his hand fondling the weapon like a lover and what was supposed to be a smile on his face. Felice drew herself up on the bed as he approached. Her mind raced; her pain almost forgotten. She did not wish to feel the power of the whip on her naked body. She recalled the welts she had seen on the bodies of the slaves; the pain she herself had felt watching Quaco, Mary, and Samson being whipped. How many lashes did *he* plan on giving her? Felice Henderson was not a slave! She was the master's daughter.

Evan was slowly removing his clothes and Felice felt panic well up inside of her as his shirt fell to the floor. His hands went to the buckle of his belt and Felice knew she did not wish to see what he had to reveal to her. His trousers dropped to the floor, the buckle of his belt making a loud 'clunk' as it hit the wood. He was left in his old, soiled drawers over which his huge belly hung.

Evan steadily approached the bed, a smirk on his face. Felice tried to steady her thoughts as she watched her captor come closer. If only she had a weapon. He stood over her, his grin one of victory. Suddenly, Felice's legs kicked out and Evan stumbled, startled.

Leaping from the bed, Felice dashed toward the door. But Evan was a quick man for his size and he reached the door before she did, blocking her exit. Raising his hand, he brought the whip down. But in this, Felice was quicker and she escaped its mighty force by ducking to the floor just in time. Evan grabbed her arm and pulled her up to him. Her hand slipped from the table which she had tried to use to steady herself.

"Who do you think you are?" he ground out. "You are nothing more than a slave. How dare you resist me?"

His face was close to hers and Felice felt overwhelmed by the scents assailing her nostrils. His arm secured her close to his body and Felice could feel what she thought was his manhood pressing against her. Her hands were pinned between them; she must get them free. Wriggling against him seemed only to inflame him so she stopped fighting. His grip on her eased somewhat and he tried to spin her around to push her back to the bed. With a mighty heave, Felice pushed him away, revealing the weapon she had secured from the table. It was a hunter's knife.

Evan did not see what was coming. Maybe he was now confident of his superior power with his whip in his hand; maybe he thought she had accepted that her resistance was futile. With as much force as she could manage with her tied hands, Felice drove the knife into his belly, a grunt escaping her. He paused as if unsure what had just happened; then his hand went to his wound. In the dim light, he examined the result of his exploration; the wetness on his fingers was his own blood. He stared at her for a moment, then back at his hand.

Felice used his moment of confusion to back away from him. He eased himself down onto the floor and the whip fell from his hand.

"What have you done?" he asked in a surprised voice.

Felice backed away from him. She was not sure how much she had hurt him but she would not wait to find out. Grabbing the handle of the door, she made her escape into the night, uncaring of her nakedness. She ran through the bushes, unsure of where she was going, dodging branches of trees and hoping she would not stumble into a pit or meet her death some other way on this night. Her breath came fast in her chest and she felt she surely would burst from her exertion.

When she thought she was far enough away, she slowed her pace and tried to see where she was. There were no other sounds in the still night except for her breath as it slowed. Using her teeth, she tugged at the cloth binding her hands until it was finally loose enough for her to pull them free. She could feel Evan's blood on her hands but dark of night shielded her eyes from the reality.

She had only traveled in a carriage or on the back of John's horse Brutus; never had she traveled unaccompanied so she had no notion of where she could be. This was not Evan's house, she knew. They had dined with him and his family on more than one occasion. Even then, she would not have been able to find her way home. Felice looked up at the night. If only she had paid more attention she would be able to use the stars to guide her home.

She must find some shelter against her nakedness, she thought as the cold night air began to penetrate her body. She would not stop until she found an abode. It did not matter which or whose. She needed to find a place of safety. Absently, she wondered if she had killed Evan. But that was not her concern at the moment. She must find shelter.

In the dark of the night, it was not easy to see but Felice found a beaten path. She kept to the edges of the road in the event that a late traveler with bad intent might stumble upon her. Or, maybe Evan had somehow recovered and had come after her. Suddenly, the road seemed familiar. She realized she was headed for Greenrock. Felice began crying as she recognized that home might not be too far away. Then, the sound of an approaching carriage caught her attention and she slipped into the bushes.

There was the sound of horses' hooves and of men's voices. She hid behind a tree. It was after the carriage passed that she recognized that a parcel of familiar men was walking behind the carriage and a few others were on mules and horses. Felice stumbled onto the road. Shouts and confusion arose and the carriage turned around. Everything seemed to become as one as Felice slumped to the earth.

Duncan Henderson climbed out of the carriage and bent to where his daughter's almost naked body lay crumpled on the road. Removing his coat, he threw it across her and lifted her into the carriage. Shouting commands to the *posse*, he turned them around and headed back toward his estate.

Felice lay shivering in one corner of the carriage. Her father sat next to her and pulled her shaking frame to his bosom, allowing her to bawl as loudly as she wanted. Her tears wet his shirt and his arms enclosed her. When she was spent, he used his handkerchief to wipe her eyes. A grim line stuck on his face, Duncan Henderson saw murder.

The carriage slowly turned into Greenrock. The estate was alive in the dark night. Cook rushed forward as Duncan Henderson alighted, lifting his daughter in his arms.

"Felice!" Cook called out, her voice somewhat tearful.

Henderson paused.

"You alright, Felice? You alright, mama baby?" Cook purred as she looked into her daughter's eyes while she lay in her father's arms.

"We must get her inside, Isabella," Henderson grunted.

"Who do dis to you, Felice?" Cook demanded.

"Isabella, not now!" Henderson ordered. "We will ask questions later. Right now, we must get her inside."

He carried Felice up the stairs with Cook following closely behind, murmuring and purring and promising judgment on whoever had caused her child harm. Duncan Henderson placed Felice on her bed and stood watching in silence as her mother sat with her. A large purple mark stood glaringly across her cheek in the candlelight. Morgie brought in a mug of tea for Felice to drink. She wiped her sister's face while Cook smoothed her hair.

"When Quaco say you gone, I never tink I could live out dis," Cook explained. "Who could do dis to you, Felice? Is not Mass John?"

"No," she responded softly.

"Who?" she demanded.

"Mr. Evan."

The room was silent except for Henderson's indrawn breath. Then Cook spoke.

"Him spoil you?" Cook whispered in her ear.

Felice was silent. How could she say 'no'? How could she when her stomach now roiled at the memory of his hands and mouth upon her flesh? Her flesh she had saved only for John. Now, Evan had spoiled that, making her feel like something soiled.

"No," she finally answered.

A collective sigh echoed around the room.

"Where him is?" Cook demanded.

"He might be dead. I stabbed him with a knife."

The room was silent. Cook looked up at her master and back at her daughter.

"Shh," Cook advised. "Doan tell nobody else, yuh hear?"

Duncan Henderson nodded at her and walked out, leaving Cook to minister to her daughter.

"Get some sleep, mi baby. You want Morgie stay wid you?"

"And you too," the girl answered simply, looking pleadingly at her mother.

Cook climbed in beside her daughter and Morgie took the other side, pulling the covers over themselves. It was like it was a long time ago when two little girls climbed into their mother's narrow bed as it stormed. They curled up under her fleshy arms and fell asleep, hoping when they woke up again the storm would have passed.

CHAPTER 11

Duncan Henderson paced the floor of the drawing room while he awaited McDowell's arrival. He had been unable to contain his anger and had taken to drinking the rum he had so avoided in an effort to calm his nerves. The blasted rum had done many a planter in and he had no intention of becoming a casualty. He had seen a number of new arrivals waste their lives and their fortunes because of that cursed liquid. But tonight, he could not help himself.

He could not believe his friend Evan, whom he had trusted, would stoop so low. It had taken all he had to not ride out in the dark of the night to exact revenge just now. But he had learned a long time ago that impulsive acts did not always have the best results. His marriage to Mary Henderson was proof of that.

A young Duncan Henderson had returned to Scotland in the year before Tacky's Revolt to settle his affairs before going back to the colony to manage his newly acquired estate. He was a man of twenty with many demons to fight and he was hoping he could leave them behind in Scotland and begin his life anew as owner of Greenrock Estate. An inheritance had left him with more money than he could hope to earn in his lifetime, thanks to an old and miserly obscure maiden aunt.

The colonies were in need of settlers then and he had taken up the call. Greenrock was starting to show promise and he realized that, even though Scotland was his home, here in the colony, he could become the master of his own destiny. So he had purchased the estate with his inheritance and determined to make it succeed.

Isabella. He knew she was with child when he left then and that he was responsible. There was just something about this dark-skinned young girl that had stirred his senses. He had not been one to throw his female slaves down and take his pleasure as was the habit of most of his peers. Isabella had been presented to him by her mother Ella as the new cook since Ella herself had been heavy with child then. Ella's child had not lived, he recalled.

There was just something about Isabella. Maybe it was the way she moved her hips in a seductive dance when she walked. Or, it could be the slant of her eyes as she took him in, her young Massa, and appreciated the sturdiness of his young frame. Or, if you believed in it, maybe it was something she put in the food she prepared for him. Although, even before he had tasted her hands, his young body had danced in a rush of heat at their first meeting. Bewitching Isabella; even after all these years, he still could not let her go. He did not see it as an act of unfaithfulness that he still found satisfaction between her legs.

Although he could not marry her, after all, she was his slave, he could make her his slave-wife. It was what was normal in the colony. What, with few white women available for a white man in the colony, a man had to take his pleasures where he could; and he had found more than pleasure between his cook's legs. She had captured his belly and his heart. Not many white women desired to leave the comforts of the motherland to live in the hot and miserable, disease-ridden colony, anyhow. So he had determined that, on his return to the colony, he would live with her as his slave-wife at Greenrock.

Back in Scotland, he had been introduced by a friend to the young and beautiful Mary Aiken and she was enraptured by his tales of the colony. He had not told her about Isabella and their child who awaited his return. Before he knew it, he had proposed marriage to Mary Aiken. Isabella and her child soon faded into darkness. It was some time before he returned to his estate to prepare for his family to live with him. By then Felice was a growing child in need of reining in as she roamed the estate with her younger sister Morgiana who had been born while he was away. He never asked who the father of this child was. It had not mattered to him. But he had heard tell that the man, from a neighboring estate, had been transported to Cuba by his owner after one of those rebellions that had followed in the wake of Tacky's revolt.

He recalled the first time he saw the golden-haired cherub that was his and Isabella's offspring. He never imagined that they could both produce such an exotic creature. He could not allow her to be a slave. He had to make her free. Now, as he thought of his daughter laying in bed, the mark of brutality on her face, he felt his anger rise again. How dare Evan lay hand in violence on Felice! How dare him! He had even paid the man for his loss when Felice had refused to be his mistress.

The sound of horses and a carriage penetrated his consciousness and Henderson left the drawing room to greet the new arrivals. Quaco opened the door to let McDowell and his son John in. John's face was a picture of anxiety.

"How is she, sir?" John asked the moment he breezed in.

"She is resting, dear boy," Henderson responded.

"May I see her?"

"Not tonight, I'm afraid, John. She needs to rest right now. She has been through an awful lot."

"Is she badly hurt then?" John continued.

"More her spirit, I believe."

John sat abruptly on the sofa and pounded a fist into his palm.

"What happened, sir?"

"Let's all sit and discuss this, shall we?" Henderson offered. "Quaco, bring us some drinks, will you?"

Quaco shuffled out and the men sat. Henderson heaved a heavy sigh.

"It seems Evan was not pleased with my daughter's refusal to be his mistress so he arranged to have her kidnapped."

John sat up, his body alert.

"Kidnapped?"

"She was on the verandah, as has become her habit after dinner. When Quaco went to lock up and advise her to turn in, she was gone. Her necklace was on the floor and there were signs of a struggle."

John let out a pained expression, his agony evident on his face.

"Did he touch her?" John ground out.

"He tried but Felice fought him off, I believe. It turns out she stabbed the bastard."

"Where is he now?" John demanded.

"Easy, boy," his father soothed. "Is he alive?"

"If he is, he will be dead soon enough," Henderson declared. "How dare he?"

"Damned out of order, if you ask me," McDowell said calmly.

There was silence in the room as each man contemplated his thoughts and what actions needed to be taken.

"We will ride over in the morning," Henderson suggested.

"I hope to God he is dead," John declared. "Or I will kill him myself."

Quaco entered with a tray of drinks which he lay out on a side table.

"A-hem," Quaco cleared his throat.

"Yes, Quaco," Henderson asked.

"Sar, Missa Evan have a lickle place eena di bush him use sometime."

"What do you mean?"

"Is mus be dere him carry Miss Felice, sah. Him sometime tek it fi sleep when him no go home."

"Are you sure now, Quaco?"

"Yes, sah. Him sometime carry woman him like dere, sah."

"Of all the..." McDowell exclaimed. "Where is this place?"

"It dung near Egypt, sah. Right as yuh ketch to di crossroad," Quaco explained.

"Thank you, Quaco. You may lock up now. Mr. McDowell and John will bunk in the guest room tonight. We will be off at light of dawn."

"Yessah."

"Here's two bits for your help."

Quaco accepted the coins from his master and shuffled out.

"Why wait until morning light?" John demanded.

"Easy, John," his father urged. "There is not much we can do tonight. We could get lost in the swamps riding around in the dark. Besides, Felice is home and safe now."

John calmed somewhat at his father's wisdom. But inside, he seethed. He wanted to place his hands around the neck of the man who had so disrespected his Felice and squeeze until there was no more sound or movement from the bastard. He wanted to plunge his dagger into that big fat belly and hear him gurgle like a pig being slaughtered. How could he sleep tonight? How could he close his eyes knowing that the dirty, rotten scoundrel was somewhere out there, having put his hands on his betrothed's flesh? The thought of Felice being touched by someone other than him made his insides churn. He hoped to God Felice had indeed killed him. Let him rot wherever he was. Morning could not come soon enough.

The sunlight filtered through the window and Felice opened her eyes. She was alone. Her mother and sister must have slipped out early to their duties. They were duties that needed to be performed no matter what.

Felice's head pounded as she sat up. Memories of the night before came rushing in on her. In the light of the day it all seemed like a bad dream. But the purple mark on her face was enough to let her know how real it had been. Her hands still bore evidence to the deed she had committed. Was Evan still alive? How much of a hurt had she caused him? She knew it was enough to let her escape from his clutches. It was Providence that had guided her to the road and into her father's arms. He had held her close and comforted her. For a few moments, she had truly felt like the master's daughter.

Her door opened and Morgie walked in with a tray. Her sister smiled at her.

"How you feel dis morning, Miss Felice?"

"My face aches."

"Doan worry. I go get you something for it. Come, drink some hot tea."

Morgie brought a mug to Felice's lips and commanded her to sip. Felice obeyed and took the mug from Morgie's hands. The steam rose over the rim and Felice blew into the liquid to cool it. After a few sips, she paused and looked at Morgie.

"Morgie, I have something to ask you."

"What it is?"

"Are you an obeah woman?"

Morgie was silent for a moment, her eyes downcast.

"What you think?"

"I don't know what to think, Morgie. I see you do things like Mino."

"Come, drink up you tea. You need fi eat too. Cook say make sure you clean off di plate."

Felice knew better than to open the discussion again. Once Morgie's mouth was shut, it stayed shut. Morgie fed her in silence and then left only to return with a salve for Felice's face.

"Missa Henderson dem gone look fi Missa Evan," Morgie said as she gently rubbed her sister's face with the foul-smelling concoction.

"Fi true?"

"Him an Missa McDowell an Mass John. Dem was here las night."

"Really? John was here?"

Felice sat up in her excitement.

"Dem sleep eena di guest room."

"I missed John," she lamented.

"Miss Felice, yuh wasn't in no condition fi see anybody last night. Now, lie back an ah will come help clean yuh up an help yuh change."

"I can't believe John was here and I did not get to see him."

"Yuh wi see him soon enough. An den yuh cyaan get him offa yuh."

Morgie chuckled.

"What do you mean by that?"

"Heh-heh," Morgie cackled. "Miss Felice, yuh will know soon enough."

"Morgie, stop talking in riddles."

"You mean yuh an Mass John doan do it yet?"

Felice stared at her sister, her meaning slowly dawning on her.

"Of course not!"

How could Morgie even think that? That was something the slaves did, unable to control their passions.

"Awright. Awright. Ah was just asking."

"Did you and Samson?"

Morgiana giggled.

"I not saying anyting. But nutting sweet like man an woman."
"Morgie! Does our mother know?"

"Maybe. I go get yuh a pail a water. Yuh still have blood pon yuh hand."

Morgie grinned at her and left the room. Felice lay back on her pillow. The salve had soothed her pain somewhat. Morgie and Samson. She had thought so but Morgie's confession made it all real. Would they now live together? It was so sad that Morgie and Samson could not have a proper wedding like she was having. She would love to see her sister in a beautiful gown and shoes on her feet and a great celebration for her and

Samson. Morgie and Samson had already crossed the line. But what did it matter when you were a slave?

Felice's own marriage was coming in a little over a fortnight. Within the week, Mary Henderson was set to return home, her quarters having been rebuilt. She was not sure if the woman would attend the wedding, but Rebecca was set to be one of her bridesmaids and young Duncan the ring bearer. Morgie and her mother would not take part.

She wished she had seen John. Although her mother and her sister had been her comfort last night, it would have been good to feel John's strong arms holding her close and his shoulder under her head. She always felt so safe around him. She wondered what her father had told him. Was John angry at Evan? What could he do? Although he was white by law, he still had no power over a white man.

Felice thought of what had almost happened to her. How could she go to John after being violated by Evan? She had to thank what Providence had intervened. When Evan had gone to fetch the whip, she had seen the knife on the table and a thought began forming in her head. He either had not seen it himself, or he had been confident that she could never reach it or think to harm him, a white man. She did not know the penalty there was for striking a white man; but she knew neither her father, nor her mother could save her. Like a cornered animal, she had waited for him to approach; and then she struck.

She did not care if he lived or died. If there was a punishment to be meted out to her, she was willing to face it rather than be dishonored by Evan. Her stomach churned at the memory of his scent and his touch. Her terror in the dark night as she ran through the bushes was still with her in the light of day. She needed John there with her to make her feel safe again. Their marriage could not come soon enough.

Morgie returned and helped Felice clean herself up. The blood had dried on her hands and she could not wait to have it completely gone. The stain left on her soul was going to be harder to erase.

Felice examined her face in the mirror. The mark across her cheek was slowly fading under the ministrations of her sister Morgie. She had been in pain for some time until Morgie prepared the salve for her. Her body ached after the trouncing it had taken being tied up on the back of a mule and being manhandled by Evan. But, Morgie had given her hideous tasting liquids to drink to help ease her pain.

She was slowly beginning to understand who Morgie was; but she worried about it being found out that she had taken Mino's place on the estate. Recalling what Mino's outcome was, she hoped her sister would not have the same fate. There was no telling what her father would do, even if Cook intervened. Obeah was against the law.

The past week had been one of difficulty for Felice. Her father, Mr. McDowell, and John had found Evan at his pen that morning. The reprobate was alive but a bit sallow in complexion. The man denied any involvement in the abduction.

"Who are you going to believe?" he inquired belligerently, "*me* or some half caste?"

"Careful, Evan. Felice is my daughter."

John stood next to his father. The dagger in his waist was begging to be drawn as he watched the man twist uncomfortably in a chair. Evan had not stood up to greet them. He claimed to be somewhat under the weather but did not elaborate on the source of his discomfort. His wife swore for him that he had not left the house the night before.

How could one accuse a white man of this level of assault? How can one accuse him of lying about committing such an act? Had it been perpetrated on a white woman then he could easily be arrested and brought to trial. But the virtue of a mulatto could never be verified; a slave, even worse. The mulattos were evidence of the depraved appetites of the planters of the colony. The men preferred their Negro slaves to the company of their English counterparts. The women lay themselves loose, seducing the men who were weakened by the intemperate climate. God knows what concoction they put in the white men's food and drink or what obeah they worked to bind themselves to them.

The mulatto woman, fit for neither Negro nor white, was fair game and could not be trusted to live a virtuous life. "Why would your *daughter* concoct such a tale?" Evan's wife asked of Duncan Henderson, her expression one of utter disgust.

Henderson stared at her in silence. He did not respond. He truly felt sorry for this woman who was privy to her husband's philandering ways but who was now defending him. He could not believe he had given it a thought to have his daughter be supported by this man. He had only thought of her future and the lack of prospects for a mulatto woman in the colony. She could marry neither a white man nor a Negro man. At least Evan, he thought, would have taken care of her; given her some children, maybe. He had promised her a house. How wrong he had been.

John's father placed a hand on his son's arm. He could sense the boy's coiled rage; and right he was to experience such anger. Had he not, McDowell would have thought it odd. His son loved the young woman and, once he had recognized that, he determined not to let anything get in the way of his son's happiness. He loved the boy and it did not matter that he was a half-caste. He was his blood; he was his future.

Although there were laws that limited inheritance by children born of liaisons such as his and Abigail's, there were ways around it. He had spent his life grooming his boy for such a day. He was glad John had found a sensible girl like Felice Henderson. She was sharp and inquisitive, even if she was something of an innocent. John would soon take care of that.

"Good day, Evan. Mrs. Evan," Henderson was saying.

John seemed ready to explode. A muscle in his jaw twitched and the veins on the sides of his head bulged. McDowell hoped he and Henderson were strong enough to hold John down should he attempt anything.

"Come on, John," he goaded as he realized his son had not turned to accompany them out.

John stood for a moment longer. Duncan Henderson approached him and touched his arm.

"John," he said softly, "We must go now. Live to fight another day."

John paused a moment more, his eyes boring into Evan's who shuffled his body as if he could not find a proper side to sit on; then he turned to accompany his father and future father-in-law outside. *This was not going to go just like that*, he promised himself.

The men left Evan's abode and, following Quaco's directions, found Evan's hut. The door was locked and they peered inside through the small window. John heaved at the structure and the door gave. There was dried blood on the wooden floor and the bed looked like it had been disturbed. Evan would probably have some reasonable explanation for the blood. He would never admit to having abducted and assaulted Felice. If Felice tried to lodge a complaint, it would be her word against his; and his word was Power.

Felice was glad to see John when he returned that morning. He had come to her room to see her. The knock on the door as she lay on her bed had startled her. She must have fallen back asleep after Morgie cleaned her up and left. Morgie had put a fresh nightgown on her; the white cotton with the pink embroidery that Cook had made for her. It was her comfort at this time.

"Come in," she called.

Her eyes opened wide as he entered.

"John!"

Rushing over to her bed, John sat on the edge and pulled her close to his bosom. She grimaced at the pain that shot through her body.

"I am so sorry, my darling," he cooed in her ear as he rocked her on his bosom.

"John, you're hurting me," she chuckled, her happiness complete.

"Sorry," he said, holding her away from him.

His hand reached up to touch her face, hovering over her bruise.

"He will pay for this," he ground out. "That bastard must pay."

"John, I'll be alright."

"No matter, Felice. He shouldn't have done this to you. I cannot imagine what you were going through."

"It was horrible, John, I have to admit. But I survived it."

"I must ask you, Felice. Did he...?"

"No."

"Good. Now get some rest. I promise I won't let you out of my sight once we are married."

He grinned at her.

"You have to at some point," she joked.

"Believe me; I will tether you to me like a goat to a fence. Felice, I am so happy you are alright. This is not over, though. Believe it."

"Oh, John. The important thing is that I am safe now."

He placed a kiss on her lips. First, it was a soft touching. Then the pressure increased and his lips moved across hers. Felice's hand reached up to the back of his head and she pulled him closer. She could feel his urgency as their kiss deepened. She heard him groan as he pulled her to him. She could feel her body aching but she did not care. She just wanted to feel him and the warmth of his body next to hers. John climbed in the bed, his lips still capturing hers, his body hovering over hers. Then, he was full length on top of her.

"Ow!" Felice uttered involuntarily.

John's leap was swift as he came to his senses.

"Felice, I am so sorry. I didn't mean to. I just got so carried away. I was just so glad to see you…"

"It's alright, John. My body just still hurts. I enjoyed our kiss."

She looked at him shyly. Her body was throbbing; but not from the pain. She recalled Morgie's comment about what went on between a man and a woman and how sweet it was. Felice had only got a small taste with the kisses they had exchanged. The promise of more had her heart beating and parts of her body aching and pulsing. Their marriage should be sooner.

John looked at her apologetically; but his eyes still burned darkly. His lips seemed to be asking for more. He stood and pulled at the bottom of his waistcoat. He explained their futile efforts to get a confession out of Evan, promising that this would not be the end of it.

Within the week, Evan's hut burned to the ground. No one could explain how the fire began. The smell of smoke filled the air and rose above the trees before anyone realized that the place was afire. It was too far from the river to fetch water on time anyway. Whatever secrets Evan held there went up in smoke and turned to ashes.

The return of Mary Henderson to Greenrock was a quiet one. Felice heard the carriage arrive as she sat on the verandah in the cool of the evening. She knew now not to stay long when it became dark. The night sky no longer held comfort for her; it brought out only the evil that walked at night, she concluded.

John and his father were set to arrive shortly for dinner. She was tired of being abed and felt much better, even though Cook was insisting that she remain in her room. It felt good to breathe the fresh air after being in confinement for the better part of a week. On top of that, there was just so much to do before the wedding took place.

Felice could hear the voices but could not make out what they were saying. Then she heard the footsteps heading for the stairs. *Well, the witch herself was back*, she thought. But somehow that did not make her feel afraid anymore. Mary Henderson no longer mattered. In a week, Felice would be a married woman and, although she would have to share a home with his mother, she took comfort in knowing that she would be John's wife.

"Hello Felice."

The voice startled her and Felice looked up at Mary Henderson. Her complexion was much healthier although she was thinner than she had ever seen her. The bones in her face seemed more defined, but somehow it complemented her.

"Mrs. Henderson," Felice greeted, standing up too quickly and feeling a little faint for it. "You are back."

"As you can see."

"How are you feeling now?"

"Much better, thank you. I hear you had a mishap."
"Yes. But I am doing better."

"Well, good luck."

Mary Henderson turned and wheeled away. Felice sat in shock. The woman could be halfway decent if she tried to be. It seemed her extended visit had done her wonders, not only in health but also in spirit. Was this the same woman who had tried to bite Felice's head any chance she got? She could be civil if she wanted to be.

When John and his father arrived, Felice was waiting. John found her on the verandah. His arms came around her and he pulled her to him.

"You get more beautiful every day," he whispered in her ear.

"And you more handsome and stronger every time I see you."

"Not much time left until you are my wife," he observed. "How are you feeling, my dear?"

"Much better, thank you. I was losing my mind being confined to my room."

He chuckled and released his hold on her.

"I hope I can make you happy," he said as he offered his hand to her.

"You have already made me so happy by wanting to marry me."

Duncan Henderson appeared at the door to the verandah.

"Time to eat," he called to them.

Hand in hand, they walked into the dining room. Mary

Henderson sat at the table, a smile pasted on her face. She was making the effort, Felice could see. Rebecca and young Duncan sat next to their mother and Felice was placed between John and his father. On John's other side was his mother who sat with her eyes downcast. Felice wished John had told her his mother would be there. The woman still was not welcoming to her.

Felice knew John's mother did not think she was good enough for her son. He had his choice of marrying a white woman, whether in the colony or in the motherland. He must have met some beautiful, eligible women in his travels there; women who perhaps came with status and money. But he had chosen her. She knew she had nothing to offer him except herself and her love in return. It made her appreciate him all the more.

Dinner was a chatty affair, mostly between the head males in the group and Mary Henderson regaling them with tales of her stay in Bluefields. The children were excited to hear of her walks along the seaside and swims in the ocean, plying her with questions she was only too glad to answer. The conversation spun around over Felice's head as she sat, one leg wrapped around John's under the table. A sudden sadness was filling her as she realized that neither her mother nor her sister could ever join them at the table. She smiled at them shyly as they served the table but was conscious that they could never partake of the fare or the conversation. They were barefooted with their heads tied with headscarves. At least John's mother, like Felice, could sit as an equal at the table.

At the end of the meal, the McDowells did not linger. It was already late and there was still much to do to prepare for the upcoming nuptials. Felice barely had a chance to say goodbye to John before they were all hurrying down the steps and out into the night. She had hoped for another lingering moment with him; but there would be other times.

As she lay in her bed that night, a feeling of excitement was building up inside Felice. Her clothes were being packed in readiness for her departure. There was nothing much left in the drawers of the bureau and on the top, except for what she needed for her daily living. This room had been her sacred place most of her life and it was hard to imagine it being empty and without her. Who would take her room when she was gone? She wished she could tell Morgie or her mother to have it; but it really was not hers to give.

A knock sounded on her door.

"Yes," she called.

Cook entered the dimly lit room with a white package in her hands. She handed it to Felice and stood watching the girl.

"What is it?" Felice inquired.

"Open it."

Felice unfolded the white cotton nightgown, which was more of a sheath. Its lacy neckline was gathered with a blue ribbon and it had small sleeves that were trimmed with lace and ribbon.

"You made it for me?"

The woman nodded.

"Wear it pon yuh wedding night."

Felice sat staring straight ahead. She could feel tears coming. Quickly, Cook sat on the edge of the bed and grabbed her daughter to her.

"What happen, Felice? Why yuh crying?"

Felice did not respond. The tears took over. How could she explain to her mother? How could she make her understand? "Mass John hurt yuh?"

"No," she said between tears.

"So wha happen? Yuh no happy?"

Felice tried to control her tears and ended up in hiccups.

"Why were you born a slave?" she finally blurted out.

Cook's body went stiff. What was her daughter saying?

"Wha yuh mean by dat, Felice?"

"It's almost like I don't have a mother. You cannot sit with us. You cannot talk with us. You cannot be a part of my wedding."

"Felice, stop di foolishness. It no matter. Me still yuh modda and Morgie still yuh sister. Nuttin can change dat."

"I know. But it is so unfair."

"Ay, mi chile. It no level at all. Jackass know dat."

"I want to see you and Morgie all dressed up, Cook. You have been my caretaker all my life. Why can't you be a part of the most important thing in my life now?"

"Felice, maybe someday tings wi different. But right now dere is two people eena di world: the massa and him slave. Yuh cyaan decide which one yuh waan fi be. Yuh born come see it an yuh haffi tek it or yuh might as just lie dung an dead. We haffi live, Felice, whedda we be massa or slave."

"I just wish it was not so."

"Ay, Felice. Is a whole heapa ting we wish fah. Me use to wish seh Massa woulda come back from Scotland an married to me. But me know it coulda nevah happen. So now, him come back wid wife an pickney, wha me go do? Me know him love me eena him way; but him will nevah leave him wife and married me. So, me tek wha me get an happy wid it. Life no fair, mi sweet baby. Life no fair at all at all."

Felice held on to her mother for a while longer. It felt almost like the last time she was going to see her. It felt like she was moving a long way off even though she was just a carriage ride away. It just did not seem fair that she had to leave her mother and sister behind to continue in their servitude just because of the accident of their births.

The week seemed to fly by in a flurry of activities. Her trunks were carried on carts to the McDowell estate. Felice looked around her bedroom. It felt empty, almost like she had died. It just seemed such a waste to have it left empty or only for guests when her mother and Morgie still slept in the cramped quarters they shared. Someday Morgie would have her own hut if she really matched with Samson. Why could she not have her room?

Mary Henderson was appearing more cheerful. Maybe it was because Felice would be leaving soon and she no longer had to come face to face each day with the result of her husband's alliance with his Negro slave. Or maybe it was because Morgie was working on healing her mistress. She boiled cabbage and fed her mistress the water. It took only a few days for the woman to stop complaining of pains and swelling in her belly. The soup she made, no one knew, except Morgie, what she put into it. But Mary Henderson looked forward each day to be fed her concoctions. Aquila looked at Morgie with suspicion. Her Missis refused to listen to her suggestions about Morgie because she was feeling so much better; almost like her old self.

The day before the wedding, the cakes were brought over to the McDowells on the heads of the slaves who walked single file, singing as they went. She had asked her father to let them attend, even if they could not take part. They had, for the most part, watched her become a woman. It would be unfair to not have them be a part of this. They had truly kept her safe, especially when Mino had tried to destroy her. They had stood as one, ready to fight for her. Her father agreed; except for the watchmen July and Potack, everyone could attend. Someone had to remain behind to make sure the estate was safe; although he was sure the men were not doing the best job of it, but what else could he do?

John's visit amid the activities that day was unexpected but welcome. He slid off his horse and handed the reins to Samson. He looked like a gentleman though his dress was casual. Felice watched his stride up the steps of the Great House toward where she stood on the verandah at the front of the house. Her body flushed with excitement. They embraced and he stood looking down into her face.

"Hello, my darling," he greeted.

Felice smiled up at him.

"I just had to see you one last time before we are wed," he continued. "I want to make sure you are alright."

"I am alright, John. There is just so much going on just now I feel like I am in a spin."

"Don't worry. Tomorrow at this time it will all be over. Is there anything you need me to do?"

"Thanks, but no. My father took care of everything."

"I wish it were today," he said as he grinned slyly at her.

"Me too. But it won't be long," Felice whispered back.

"I will be off, then. So, I will see you in the morning?"

"Try and stop me."

She watched him leap onto his horse, wishing she were alongside him; that, like the slaves, they did not need a piece of paper to show their love for each other. But, tomorrow. As Cook would always say, "tomorrow like now, we eena tiger fat." John gave a small salute as he turned his horse and rode down the hill, kicking up a small cloud of dust behind him.

Felice awoke on her wedding morning with two bodies next to her. They had lain awake most of the night. Their conversations had brought them back to long ago times when Morgie and Felice would run the estate with the other slave children who were not yet ready for the fields. Cook reminded Felice of a day when the little girl had tried to pick up the baby fowls and the mother hen had come after her. Felice's memory of this was somewhat hazy, but she was sure her mother had saved her then.

They giggled like little girls at the memory of their antics in the time of innocence. Then one of them fell asleep, they could not recall which one. The night grew silent as the three women finally gave in to the land of slumber.

The wooden bath was brought in and Cook and Morgie assisted Felice with her bath. Morgie crushed some bushes between her palms and placed them in the water. A pleasant scent rose in the room.

"What is that, Morgie? Some of your obeah?" Felice joked.

"Felice, I am not a obeah woman," Morgie said in a soft but firm tone. "I am a healer. I know di right herbs to use for healing. Never you call me a obeah woman again."

"I'm sorry, Morgie."

"Dat is lavender bush. It take away yuh worries. Mek yuh calm like a lamb," Morgie explained.

"How you know these tings, Morgie?" Felice asked her sister.

"I jus know. Come mek we get yuh ready fi Mass John. Felice, yuh is a lucky girl."

They bathed her in the lavender scented water and dried her off before seating her in front of the mirror, wrapped in a towel. Cook took the brush and began brushing her daughter's hair almost absently. Felice's eyes met hers in the mirror and the girl could almost swear she saw a tear at the corner of her mother's eye. But Cook blinked and smiled at her. The women piled the girl's hair on top of her head and secured it with a decorative pearl and silver hair comb.

Quaco's Mary entered the room to make her face up. Felice had not seen the woman since the last time she and Morgie had gone to help her with her fever.

"Miss Felice, the time come, eeh?" Mary commented. "Yuh ready to be a woman?"

Felice giggled.

"Mary!" she protested.

"Well, we all woman here," Mary continued. "Is a road we all mus walk one time or anodda. I hope Mass John tek care a

yuh, ma'am. I coulda nevah ask fah anyone betta dan my Quaco. Him is a good man. Miss Felice, tek care a Mass John an him wi tek care a yuh. Das all dere is to it."

Her job done, Mary stood back to survey her work. The dark mark on the girl's cheek was almost faded, hidden beneath the white mask of the cosmetics painted on her face. Mary smiled in satisfaction. The bride simply glowed, her cheeks rosy from the pink rouge. It was time to get Felice into her gown.

Her dress was a blue gown gathered in pleats at the front and with mid length ruffled sleeves. Felice had tried it on once when it had arrived almost a fortnight before. Now, with her hair done and face made up, she almost did not recognize the doll-like creature looking back at her from the mirror. She recalled the Christmas ball and how different she had looked then, all dressed up. The women smiled, proud of their handiwork.

"Mass John gwine be a happy man today," Cook commented.

The sudden sound of singing reached her ears and Felice hurried to her window. It seemed all the slaves on the estate were gathered beneath the window and were smiling up at her. She waved down at them. She was not sure what they were singing but she felt her heart thump in her chest. This they were doing for her. It was her wedding morning. It was time to head over to her new home for the wedding breakfast and to become the bride of John McDowell.

Felice hurried down the stairs assisted by her mother and sister. The carriage waited, almost completely covered with flowers. Even the horse wore a wreath of flowers. Samson stood in his livery at the door of the carriage, his feet shod. Felice glanced at her mother and sister as if for reassurance.

"Doan worry. We soon come."

Samson assisted Felice into the carriage and, amid cheers and shouts, she was off to where John waited, perhaps impatiently. Her eyes roved all around at the passing scenery. Samson did not seem to be in a hurry. It was as if he was giving her one last chance to say goodbye to the life she knew. What awaited her in this new life she was embarking on? She felt a moment's trepidation; then, she shook it off. There was no time for that now. There was no turning back. A thrill coursed through her.

A welcoming plaited coconut branch arch decorated with flowers greeted their carriage as they arrived at the McDowell's estate. A cheer went up from the slaves who awaited them. Felice peered out at the sea of faces of every shade of dark, welcoming her home. She did not know any of them; they would now call her 'Missis'. The carriage pulled up at the front of the Great House and Duncan Henderson came out to meet his daughter.

He looked distinguished in his grey coat, waistcoat, and breeches. He extended a hand to help her out of the carriage. Felice smiled up at him.

"You look absolutely stunning, my dear," he remarked as she took his hand.

He escorted her to the drawing room where Rebecca and young Duncan waited patiently. Mary Henderson sat on a sofa, a mass of curls piled on her head. Felice thought that must be a wig the woman was wearing. John's mother stood surveying her from her position next to an armchair. Felice smiled at her and the woman moved her lips as if attempting to smile back. But Felice no longer cared. In a few moments she would be married to this woman's son; it did not matter if she liked her or not.

"Where is John?" Felice asked of no one in particular.

"Do you not know that it is bad luck for the bride and groom to see each other on the wedding day?" Mary Henderson answered.

Felice was directed to a chair on which she sat. It seemed long moments before anyone said anything and she wasn't sure what she should do next. What were they waiting for?

And then she heard them; the voices of the slaves from Greenrock singing as they arrived. They must have walked the distance between the estates. Felice could imagine her mother and Morgie walking proudly at the head of the procession, bringing gifts for the bride and groom. She wished they had been able to ride with her in the carriage.

"We can now begin," McDowell announced.

Felice was guided to the hallway where she could see the slaves all gathered with baskets and other bundles on their heads for the newlyweds. Mary Henderson fussed over her as if she were her mother. Was she so glad to be rid of Felice? Her father stood next to her and smiled reassuringly at her. She could feel the flutters in her stomach as she wondered where John was and if he himself was feeling the same way she was.

It felt like a dream as she walked beside her father and entered the drawing room where John awaited. Their eyes locked and she could see the appreciative look as his eyes took in her form. She loved him so. He was so handsome in his cream-colored wedding suit with its waistcoat, long coat, and breeches. He wore a white shirt that was ruffled at the sleeves, and a neck cloth.

Felice heard her own voice as if from afar as she promised to love and obey her husband for all her life. John promised he would forsake all else and care only for her. And then it was done. Just like that.

Felice McDowell. She made her mark in the register for the last time as Felice Henderson.

The wedding breakfast was spread out in the dining room. There was ham, fish, beef, and pork accompanied by a variety of vegetables, ground provisions, and cassava, tea, cocoa, and coffee. Breakfast became a luncheon with food from both estates. Felice loved the *duckonoo* made by the slaves who competed to prove which estate made the best. Some were made using bananas and spices; others using sweet potatoes, all wrapped and tied in banana leaves and boiled.

And then a dinner as everyone celebrated the union. The slaves had their own celebration outside in the yard. They had plaited coconut branches to form booths where they ate and drank while they sang and danced. Men lopped off the tops of the coconuts with their bills and passed them around. Some tipped a little rum inside the liquid, throwing their heads back as they guzzled, their bellies satisfied. Their chatter and laughter were incessant. Inside the Great House was its own celebration and the ballroom was opened for invited guests, not to include the slaves, to make merry.

John held Felice firmly to his side. He was keeping her tethered as he had promised as if he feared that somehow she might be snatched from him. He could hardly wait for later that night to hold her closer still.

"If only my mother and sister could come inside," Felice lamented to John.

"Should I talk to my father?" he asked.

"Will it be alright?"

"We will never know until we try."

Dragging Felice behind him, John hurried off to find his father. His father agreed that for a few minutes Isabella and Morgiana could enter his abode to congratulate the bride and groom. Felice was ecstatic as she hurried off to find them, dragging her new husband behind her.

Cook and Morgie were sitting on the grass, their legs crossed as they ate. They placed their food on the ground and stood.

"Miss Felice," Cook greeted.

"Mr. McDowell says you may come inside," she announced, a wide grin across her face.

"Why?" Morgie asked.

"Because I want you both to."

"I doan know, Miss Felice."

"It is alright, right John?"

John nodded and the women looked at each other. They followed Felice and John up the steps. They were dressed in their best gowns and their feet clad in cast off slippers. Felice could not recall ever seeing their feet shod before; their gait, however, was not awkward. The women stood in awe as they entered the hallway. All around were gaily dressed men and women moving about. Felice directed them into the dining room and all activity stopped. She brought them over to the table and bade them partake.

John's mother frowned from her position at the head of the table. All eyes were on the women as they gazed at the wide array of food laid out fit for a king and queen. Duncan Henderson appeared at their side.

"Help yourselves, Isabella. Morgie. There's more than enough. It is your daughter's wedding feast, after all."

The room was silent, watching. Cook grabbed a plate and handed one to Morgie. If this was the only time they would eat like queens then so be it. They piled their plates at Henderson's direction and moved to the verandah where they sat on the floor. Today was the day they would dine with the Massas. Today, they would taste the Massa's fare and not just what was left over once the table was cleared. Today, they would feel like they were free, even for a moment, and were equal to the people of the Great House.

The merriment continued until it grew dark and Greenrock's slaves silently trooped back to their abodes and their enslavement. It was not often that they felt this free. It was not often that they mingled with the Massa and his equals. Felice hugged her mother and sister. She watched her father and his family ride away. Then, a silence descended on the Great House and Felice realized that she was finally alone with her husband. Greenrock was no longer her home.

John's arm came around her shoulder as they stood at the top of the steps watching the last of the guests leave. The estate slaves were cleaning up and getting ready to lock up. The booths would quite likely remain for a few days until they started falling down or were no longer fresh and green.

"Can you believe it?" he whispered to her.

"We are wedded, John," Felice responded softly.

He led her up the stairs and to his quarters. At the door of his suite he turned the knob and paused.

"May I?" he asked as he smiled at her.

Swiftly, he lifted her off her feet and carried her across the threshold before depositing her on her feet on the other side.

"Welcome home, Mrs. McDowell," he said with a small bow.

Felice moved toward him. He reached out to her and in a moment she was swept up in his kiss. His lips were gentle as if he were exploring; then, their pressure increased and the kiss became more intense. Felice felt her heart flutter as his hands began roving her body.

"My darling," he whispered when he finally released her lips from his. "You taste so sweet."

His hand came to the ribbon of her dress and loosened it. Then he removed her dress and stood for long moments taking in her young form. Seemingly satisfied at what he was seeing, he lifted her and walked toward the bed where he gently laid her. Felice felt so strange lying there without her clothes having his eyes graze over her form. But, stranger still was the way her body was aching to feel him.

He dragged off his waistcoat, having long discarded his coat and cravat in the course of the evening. Pulling off his breeches, he joined her in the bed. John pulled her to his bosom and held her for a moment. Then his hand began caressing her.

Felice did not know that a man's hands could bring her so much pleasure. As he kissed her, he whispered loving words to her each time his lips left hers. His mouth then began trailing her body until it found her nipples. Felice uttered cries of pleasure and satisfaction as the thrills ran through her. She tried not to recall the distasteful touch of another who had almost violated the body meant only for her husband's touch.

Her body pulsed and she ached for him; but she was afraid. Morgie had told her it hurt the first time but that it was only feelings of pleasure after that. His hand moved to open her legs and she resisted.

"What is it, my darling?" he asked.

"I am a little afraid," she responded, her head buried in his shoulder.

"I will be gentle with you, my virgin wife. I won't hurt you, I promise."

Felice knew she could not turn back now. She longed to feel the pleasure his touch and kisses were promising her. She longed for him to finally make her a woman. She could not control the way her body wanted to be claimed as his wife in every way.

She cried out softly and then the pain was over. She was now a woman. She was now wife of John McDowell in every way. He cradled her to him, both arms wrapping her tightly as he rained soft kisses on her forehead. Thus, he fell asleep.

Felice lay in a state of half wakefulness listening to her husband's soft snores. Her body felt at peace. As she drifted off to sleep, wrapped in her husband's arms, she realized how much her life had changed. She was no longer just the master's daughter; she was now someone's wife. Mrs. John McDowell.

In the last waking moments she remembered the nightdress her mother had made her. She smiled. She had really not needed it.

The morning sun peeped into the room where Felice and John lay wrapped together in their nakedness. Sometime during the night, his body had found hers and had wrapped itself around her. Felice tried to move but he held her fast.

She glanced around her at the strangeness of the room. Although she had been there before, it was a strange sight for her to not wake up to see her own bureau and wardrobe. She wondered where her things were.

The memories of the day and night before came flooding back to her and she smiled. She stretched her hand out to look at her wedding band; it seemed to glint at her in the morning light.

"What are you looking at, Mrs. McDowell?" John's voice came to her from somewhere above her head.

She had not realized he was awake. Felice smiled again.

"That thing that binds me to you," she remarked.

"Is it a good binding?"

"Yes. So far."

John reached out and turned her face up to his. Felice felt somewhat shy as she recalled the way he had loved her the night before; the things he had said to her in the moments when his passion came. She felt his hands roving her body and her flesh tingled at his touch. His eyes held her gaze; a small smile was on his lips. He planted a soft kiss on her lips.

Then he moved his body to lay on top of hers, cradling her head in his palm.

"You are so beautiful, my darling wife. I cannot imagine not having you as my wife."

Felice smiled at him and he rained gentle kisses on her face. Her heart thumped wildly as her body began an aching, a longing to feel him again. His mouth moved down her neck in a trail of kisses, his tongue creating a magical path down to her bosom. Then his lips enclosed a nipple and Felice heard herself gasp and moan at the sensations he was awakening in her body.

The night before was an exploring of their love, Felice somewhat unsure of what to expect mostly because of the pain she did not know. Now, as John devoured her body, she awakened to how a woman could need a man and a man a woman. There was no pain; only pleasure as he finally came to her, filling her so completely she felt like she could cry.

They could remain in bed together forever; but someone's stomach grumbled as they lay wrapped together, satisfied in both their bodies and souls. They giggled.

"Was that you?" he asked.

"No. I think that was you," Felice responded on a giggle.

"It seems we two have truly become one," he remarked with a chuckle.

Releasing her, John rose from the bed.

The Master's Daughter   Vjange Hazle

"I will have a tray brought up, my dear. You remain in bed while I take care of you."

Felice wrapped herself up in the sheets while he dressed himself. She watched him pull his trousers on over his naked bottom. She liked the firmness of him. She liked the way his hair was tousled first thing in the morning. She like the way he stood tall against the frame of the window. He pulled on a shirt and smiled at her. Bending over, he planted a quick kiss on her lips before exiting the room.

She lay back on the pillows and looked up at the ceiling, wondering what was going on back at Greenrock. It was so strange not being able to run down the stairs to where her mother worked busily to feed the occupants of the Great House. Or go find Morgie for a quick talk or just to bother her. Or bump into her father or Mary Henderson for that matter on her way to breakfast. Her whole life had changed and she must now get used to living a new way of life.

For seventeen years she had been the master's daughter. She had been caught between two worlds, not knowing where she belonged. It had taken some time for her to find her place. She had been tossed between being the daughter of the master and being the daughter of a slave, and had finally settled into the in-between space that was her existence. Now, she wondered what her new life with John would be.

There was a knock on the door before it opened and a woman entered with a pitcher of water. Felice gasped.

"Morgie!" she squealed in disbelief and with a note of excitement.

"Good morning, Miss Felice," her sister greeted with a smile.

"What are you doing here?" Felice asked as she sat up in the bed.

"Missa Henderson hire me out fi stay wid you for a little."

Felice wanted to rush to Morgie with a hug; but she was conscious of her naked state beneath the covers. Morgie poured water from the pitcher into the basin.

"You going to get up or what, Mistress McDowell?" Morgie asked with a grin. "Or you too tired."

Felice grinned wickedly at her sister.

"Morgie! Morgie!" she exclaimed suggestively and giggled.

"Don't I tell you? Mek me see di sheet."

Morgie pulled the sheet away and, sure enough, there was a red spot where Felice had slept. Felice gasped. Morgie smiled.

"Come, Miss Felice. Get yuhself clean up an change. Mass John ordering something fi yuh eat."

Morgie was back to her usual business as she fussed around her Missis, pulling out a dress and some underclothes for Felice to change into. Felice wiped herself down, feeling somewhat tender between her legs. Morgiana helped Felice to put on her dress just in time. A knock sounded at the door and John entered the room.

"Good morning, Mass John," the girl greeted as she curtsied.

"Good morning, Morgiana. How are you this morning?"

"Awright, Mass John. Ah hope yuh had a good rest, sah."

"Like a baby. Felice, my dear, Martha will be up shortly with a meal for us. I see you have changed."

"Yes. It seems my father has sent Morgie to assist me in the next few days."

"Good. Welcome, Morgie."

Morgie's face was wreathed in smiles. She could now set her mother's heart at ease that her daughter was well and seemed happy. The smile was still on her face as she exited the room. A tall, slender mulatto man entered as Morgiana exited. He carried a pitcher of water in his hand and a towel over his arm.

"Missis," he said gently, bowing at Felice where she sat on a stool at the bureau.

"My dear, this is my man Mulatto John," her husband introduced.

Another Mulatto John? What was *his* story, she wondered. Felice acknowledged the man who busied himself preparing his master's toilette.

The mulattos were everywhere it seemed, Felice thought. Locked in her own world, she was not aware of how many there were in the colony. They had visited other estates and plantations and she had seen some. But, it was at the Christmas ball that she had seen a whole class of them. They belonged in their own world even as they crossed worlds.

She thought of John's mother and her status as the 'wife' of Mr. McDowell. Now, here, another mulatto was serving as helper to someone who would be considered his kind. Some mulattos, she had discovered, were themselves enslaved because their fathers refused to acknowledge their parentage or to set them free. She blessed her own good fortune that her father had taken her in so that she would not have to live in enslavement.

Food was brought up to the room and she and John dined off the trays provided as they sat on the floor at the end of the bed. He fed her fruits and spooned porridge into her mouth as they reclined on the pillows taken from the bed. They tasted each other again until they were exhausted but exhilarated where they lay on the floor. At the sound of a knock on the door, they both announced 'enter' in unison, quickly sitting up and adjusting themselves. They burst out in giggles.

In the doorway stood John's mother. Felice rose quickly but John's hand came up to pull her down.

"Mother!" John exclaimed.

Felice smiled up at her.

"I've come to change the sheets," she explained.

"You could have sent Martha to do that, Mother," John protested.

She did not respond but advanced into the room toward the bed. Removing the sheets, she paused before rolling them up into a bundle.

"I will send Martha in with some clean ones," she said as she left the room, the white bundle in her arms.

"I don't know why she doesn't like me," Felice lamented when the door closed.

"She will get to like you soon enough," John consoled.

"I don't think she ever will. She does not think I am good enough for you."

John turned to face her.

"My darling, listen to me. You are now Mrs. John McDowell. You have as much right to be here as my mother. Do not, I repeat, do not ever make her feel she has the upper hand on you. She is my mother and I love her dearly. But you are my wife and future mother of my heir. You have to stand up strong to her."

Felice thought back to Cook's advice on dealing with Mary Henderson. The difference was that Mary Henderson was a white woman. No matter what, she would always have the upper hand. But, how was she going to live in the same house with this woman? How, when this was her house long before Felice was born?

"Come," John said as he rose and extended a hand to her. "I will take you on a tour of the estate. One day I will teach you how to ride."

"I would love that," she responded, longing to be able to ride again with him in the dark of the night where they could claim their power.

He pulled her up to his chest and placed a kiss on the tip of her nose.

"I love you so," he declared, his brown eyes twinkling as they met her grey ones.

Felice was awed by the vastness of the McDowell estate. Someday, she thought, this could be hers and John's. It was indeed strange how her life had changed. Her future was laid out before her and she smiled at the thought of living it with John. Some day they would have children and their children would have their own children. Their legacy could go on forever.

She thought of Cook and Morgie and all the other slaves. Maybe some day they would get the freedom they so longed for and become masters and mistresses of their own destinies. Maybe they would remain in servitude forever; after all, some said that the Negro was born to serve. Would they keep on fighting for that freedom? Or would they finally give up their quest to settle into the space carved out for them? Their future was unclear.

As she gazed across the expanse of fields where some worked, backs bent double under the threat of a master's whip, Felice was glad she was not one of them. At least, she knew what her future was. After all, no matter what, she would always be the master's daughter.

The Master's Daughter		Vjange Hazle

Postlude

The Master's Daughter   Vjange Hazle

Western Jamaica, British West Indies, 1778

Abenaa glanced around her at the faces of the men staring at her naked body and talking amongst themselves. She did not understand what they were saying but she knew it was about her. Others had gone before her and similarly examined. Now it was her turn to stand on the wooden box. The others had not returned after they were led away from the ship so she supposed that this was the end of their journey.

Her dark youthful skin glistened in the sun as she stood on the deck of the vessel that had brought her many days across the sometimes tossing ocean. The palm oil they had rubbed over her body made her skin glow in its blackness. Her playmate Adwoa had not survived the crossing. Abenaa had wept for her in the dark belly of the vessel; but no arms had come to comfort her. There were no drums for Adwoa as she made her way to her ancestors.

A pale man with a large girth approached her. His breath made her stomach feel like the few contents in it were about to come up. It was nothing compared to the dark putrid gut of the vessel where people died and were not removed until someone came down to bring them up for some air and light. It was nothing compared to the smell of filth and other body actions that occurred because it was a human function. Abenaa held her head down as the man walked around her.

The man's hand came to her chin and forced her face up. For a moment, her eyes met his and she felt a strange shiver go through her body. He looked at her as if she would be his next meal. His hands touched her young body, lingering on her small breasts and pulling at her nipples. Abenaa stood still, trying to understand the sensations that went through her at his touch. He grinned, displaying stained teeth. She looked back down at the floor of the vessel, feeling like she was being prepared to be devoured.

She had seen lions and other animals devour their prey and she was sure that, before the end of the day, she too would lay a bloodied mess like a gazelle or a zebra. Adwoa was truly fortunate that she would not know this fate. They had thrown her now useless body overboard. The man made some gestures to the captain of the vessel and soon the two men were standing close, heads bowed as they engaged in discussion. They exchanged papers and shook hands.

Abenaa and Adwoa had been playing with the other children of the village when, suddenly, there were shouts. Some had escaped; but Abenaa and her friend Adwoa were not of those. They had been easy to carry, twelve years old with their woman's body just beginning to form. Shackled together, they had shuffled along through bushes and across grassy fields until they came to the big river. They had slept and awakened in places unfamiliar to them. Tired and worn, their feet bloody and hurting, they had finally had a chance to rest when they were marched down into the dank dungeon of the castle.

But the rest did not bring them respite as they waited. Adwoa became ill with a cough and seemed to be getting weaker. Abenaa fretted for her that her friend would die. But Adwoa was a tough one. The day they were brought up from the dungeon, Adwoa's spirits revived. Perhaps she thought they would return to their village. Instead they were brought through a portal where the big river, the one with no end, lay before them. Abenaa felt a panic she had never known before in her young life. She thought of her mother, father, brothers, and sisters.

Would she ever see them again? Were her brothers and sisters even now back to playing in the village like they used to? Or were they now mourning the death of their beloved Abenaa and her friend Adwoa? She could not tell how much time had passed since she had been with them. They must have given up hope by now for her return to them.

She knew the river outside their village that they were told by their elders not to swim in contained crocodiles and snakes that could devour in one swallow. Too often an inattentive child who had gone to draw water had been dragged into the watery depths, never to return. Now, this big river must surely swallow them up even if the creatures that lived there did not.

"Don't worry, Abenaa," Adwoa cooed. "If those pale men came across that great river, then it is possible we won't be killed in it."

Abenaa smiled grimly at the wisdom of her young friend. She did not know what awaited them on the other side of the river; the one that seemed to never end. But Adwoa was right. Abenaa kept her fear hidden as they were lowered in boats and rowed toward the large vessel that awaited them. There was a wailing as the coast of their home moved away and they were herded like animals to the hold of the vessel.

Many had awaited the day they would be brought on deck to be washed down and exercised; and unchained. Often, they were forced to dance at the cracking whip while the men laughed at their plight as if at a sport. It had become too much for some. A swift dash and a leap over the sides of the vessel was all it took and they would be swallowed up forever in the deep waters. Others, like Adwoa, would never see the sunlight again before they went to their ancestors. Adwoa's cough had not got better. She was found one morning with the dried blood on her face, her head hanging from the berth she shared with Abenaa. Abenaa had not heard when her friend's coughing stopped in the dark of night. Adwoa would never know how it was to be torn apart and eaten by the man who now stood before Abenaa.

Days on end they were tossed upon the waters. Abenaa had seen the water rise to great heights and come crashing on the vessel. Then, the pale men would shout and scurry about, forgetting their charges. It was a time many made a rush for the sides, uncaring they were chained to another, and jumped overboard. That had happened only once. More often, Abenaa had been in the belly, being pitched from body to body, rolling in the contents of another's stomach, or staring into the sightless eyes of one who had silently slipped away, answering the call of the ancestors.

Removing the shackles, the captain pushed Abenaa toward

the man who nodded to a dark man who looked like her. Abenaa looked up at this new man with hope in her eyes. But, roughly, he grabbed at her hand and led her away to a waiting cart. He threw a garment at her and had her put it on before shoving her to the wagon. There was already a man and a young boy sitting on the floor of the wagon. The clothes they wore, it was evident, did not belong to them. Abenaa felt her eyes fill. She was all alone and did not know where she was being taken to.

All around her were other pale men and some dark men going about their various businesses. They all spoke in a tongue she did not understand. Always, it was the pale men shouting commands to the dark men. She looked up at the sky. It was the same as the one she looked at in her village. Maybe this journey had brought her back to her village. Maybe she was going home.

The wagon bumped along the rutted paths and Abenaa felt her body must surely break into pieces. The man and boy spoke in their own tongue. Abenaa shifted her body, hoping to find a better way to sit. After the reprieve of being fed and oiled, it felt like she was back on the ship.

Suddenly, the man and the boy leaped from the moving wagon and into the surrounding bushes. There was a shout as the driver realized what had occurred and leaped from the front seat of the wagon. The man who had bought her also leaped from his seat and they both headed into the bushes at a run.

Abenaa wondered if she too should make her escape. But, where would she go? Would she be better off taking her chances being eaten by some wild animal in this strange place? How different would that be from what awaited her at the end of the journey? She glanced around her. She could hear the shouts. Abenaa quickly scrambled to her feet and jumped off the wagon onto the ground.

"Stay *right* there!" a voice shouted.

She did not understand the tongue but knew she had been told to halt. A pistol was pointed directly at her. The man who had bought her stood holding the boy with one hand; the other hand aimed the weapon at her. The other man held the older prisoner fast. Abenaa climbed back into the wagon and the men proceeded to tie her traveling companions against the side.

Ripping the shirts off their backs, the man removed the whip that was used for the mule. He raised his arm and came down with all his might with the whip to their backs in turn. The boy wailed at the first blow. The man spoke harshly to him in their tongue and the boy whimpered until he could take no more. He began howling again. Abenaa stared in horror at the bloodied backs.

Finally, the whipper ceased his labor. Together, he and the other man lifted the victims and threw them onto the floor of the wagon where they each landed with a thud. Abenaa tried not to look at the men's wounds. Her stomach churned. She had seen men wounded. Her mother had taken care of wounded men. But never had she seen men wounded like this. She had seen animals being torn to pieces before being eaten. A fear ran through her. Was this now, surely their fate?

The boy groaned. The man laying next to him turned his head away and lay there in his silence as if a storm was agitating in his belly. Abenaa could see the blood running down their sides and onto the floor of the wagon.

The wagon finally turned onto a path that led to a house. It was by no means a large house; but to Abenaa it was more than she was used to. She could smell the animals kept there and could see men and women engaged in various tasks. They glanced up as the wagon pulled up to the front of the house and then went back to their tasks.

"Nellie," the man called to a woman who was sweeping the steps with a handful of bushes.

"Yes, Missa Evan," she responded as she came forward.

"Take this one in hand," he commanded. "Her name is Mary. She is your responsibility."

"Yes, sar," Nellie answered.

Abenaa was handed off to the woman Nellie. She was a tall woman with a long face and a straight nose; but her face was marked on one cheek. Abenaa did not know then that she too would soon be branded as property of her owner. She did not know then that she was now a slave and that freedom from servitude would be a long time coming. She did not know then that she would not live to tell the tale nor sing the songs of freedom when it finally came to the colony.

Mr. Evan's eyes were sunken in their sockets. His belly rumbled in a cesspool of bitterness. His mouth tasted like bitter gall. Dr. Bayly had come and gone. The man had bled him and mumbled something about never seeing anything like this before. Mrs. Evan stood straight-backed, watching her husband where he lay in his bed.

Three days before, he had fallen from his horse while returning from the fields. The horse had simply buckled under him, it seemed, and they had to put it down. When his men found him, he was bleeding from a wound on his head. But there was nothing to indicate what had caused his injury. He had fallen on earth and there were no rocks or anything else present that could have caused his wound. He could not tell what had occurred or who had passed his way that day, stopping him in his path. There were whispers but no one was saying whose shadow they had seen pass by as Evan rode proud atop his horse, a whip in his hand.

"Shadow! Shadow!" were the words he uttered, his hands gesturing as if to shield his eyes.

He had not eaten in those three days. Falling into his bed, he had not been able to get up or speak after that. How could a man so strong be brought this low so quickly? He seemed to be at death's door.

Mary, the new slave girl entered. Mrs. Evan looked at her quickly. She still did not understand why her husband had even bought this one. She was too young and was useless for the hard work that was done on the Pen. She could not milk a goat if her life depended on it. But, a suspicion had formed quickly in the woman's mind.

It was not that she did not know of her husband's proclivity for young untouched women, whether enslaved or free. She recalled not too long ago when Henderson's mulatto daughter had attacked him with a knife. When his men had brought him home bleeding, she had done all in her power to save him. She should have let him bleed to death then.

But, his success was her success. Being the wife of a Pen keeper was no glamorous position to be in. The stink of animals was always in her hair and in her clothes. It was in the food she ate. It was in the house the slaves constantly cleaned and aired. The perpetual noises the creatures made, especially in the night when everyone was abed, had almost driven her mad in the beginning. They were always shoving shit at the pen. It was not like the sugar estate where everything was far away from the Great House where the master lived or the coffee or pimento plantation where the scents permeating the air were pleasant and welcoming. But, at least she could lord it over the slaves and other whites who hired themselves out for work. She was glad she was not one of them.

The girl stood over Evan and he raised weak eyes to her face.

The girl had arrived only four months before. Her thin form had blossomed quickly into a fullness that was not sitting well with Evan's wife.

"I've made arrangements for your child to be free, if anything happens to me," he assured.

His wife's gasp was audible in the silence of the room. He had not spoken since his confinement.

That night, a figure ran through the darkness shouting "Shadow! Shadow!" The speed at which the large man moved was much for his size. Among the trees and bushes he plunged. No one followed him as he continued his cry. He fell with a splash into the river; a splash heard only by himself and the other night creatures. A *Patoo* hooted as if in response.

With morning light came the discovery that Mr. Evan was gone from his bed. There were whispers that he had gone down to the river. A search was made but no one found him. Three days later, he was found, his body swollen beyond recognition.

Abenaa, hands on her small belly, did not weep for him. Neither did his wife. When the news came of his demise, Cook smiled and uttered a word no one had heard her say before. Duncan Henderson looked at her in shock as he delivered the information. She had said what he had wanted to vocalize. John McDowell sat back in his chair listening to his father talk about the death of Evan. He was silent, a feeling of satisfaction settling over him. He gently squeezed his Felice's hand. The news spread. That night there was the sound of drums and voices raised in song as if a celebration.

The colony had claimed another victim.

About the Author

Vjange Hazle was born in Jamaica and migrated to the United States in 1989. She began publishing in the 1980s in the *Gleaner's* Sunday Magazine and later in the Caribbean magazine *Focus* 1983. Her short stories have also been published in *The Caribbean Writer-Volume 4* and *New Writing from the Caribbean* edited by Erika J. Waters. Her stories and poetry have also appeared in numerous other publications. In 2004, she published *country gal a foreign-Volume 1*, a collection of stories which first appeared in *The West Indian-American Newspaper* in Hartford, CT as *Chit-Chat*. A graduate of Mico Teachers' College (now Mico University College) in Jamaica, she holds a Bachelor of Arts degree in English from Eastern Connecticut State University, a Master of Arts in Communication from the University of Hartford, and a Master of Arts in English from Central Connecticut State University.

The Master's Daughter   Vjange Hazle